"Are you trying to drown your sorrows?"

Jodan moved closer to Kasey, "If that's the case, I can vouch for the fact they'll all be there tomorrow."

Sorrows? He didn't know the half of it. How would he feel if his life had been shattered like hers? What could this stranger—anyone—do?

"Tell me about it." His deep, soft voice broke in on her thoughts. "Maybe I can help."

Kasey drew herself together. "You can't. No one can. Unless you know someone who's looking for a wife."

Had she actually said that? Or just thought it? Their eyes met, rusty brown and light blue.

"As a matter of fact, I do," he said evenly, holding her gaze. "How about me?"

LYNSEY STEVENS, an Australian author, has a sense of humor that adds a lively quality to her writing. She has always enjoyed her work as a librarian—in a modern library providing children's activities, puppets, theater and other community services—but her first love is writing. Though her earlier attempts at writing historical and adventure novels were unsuccessful, and her first romance novel was rejected, Lynsey now has several published books to her credit. And she hints at the presence of a real, live Harlequin hero in her life.

LYNSEY STEVENS

a rising passion

Harlequin Books

TORONTO • NEW YORK • LONDON
AMSTERDAM • PARIS • SYDNEY • HAMBURG
STOCKHOLM • ATHENS • TOKYO • MILAN

For my sister, Lana.
Many thanks for your help and support.

Harlequin Presents first edition September 1991
ISBN 0-373-11396-X

Original hardcover edition published in 1990
by Mills & Boon Limited

A RISING PASSION

CHAPTER ONE

IT MUST have been well after eight p.m. when a knock on the door of the flat she shared with a friend from her schooldays took Kasey by surprise. Who on earth would be calling at this time on a Saturday evening? All the acquaintances she had in Sydney would be out at some party or other and wouldn't be making a friendly neighbourly call.

Pushing her russet hair back from her face, she grimaced ruefully at the faded jeans and old sweatshirt she wore. The relaxing Kasey Beazleigh. Far removed from the up-and-coming model Katherine Claire Beazleigh.

She crossed the room, and when she put her eye to the peephole her legs nearly gave way beneath her. She fumbled with the chain and her fingers seemed loath to work properly in her haste to open the door.

'Hi, Kasey! I expected you'd be out, seeing as it's Saturday night.' He shifted uncomfortably, twisting his broad-brimmed hat in his hands. 'I was going to wait until the morning, but——' His eyes seemed to be devouring her. 'Can I come in?'

Kasey stepped aside, sure she was dreaming.

'How are you?' His eyes moved over her as she closed the door behind him.

'I'm fine.' Her voice sounded hollow, as though it were coming from a long way off, and she swallowed quickly.

Greg was here. He'd come at last. The realisation began to filter through the foggy confusion of her disbelief. He'd come to tell her his engagement to Paula was off. That had to be the reason.

A spurt of happiness surged up inside her and she put out her hand to him. 'What are you doing in Sydney?'

Greg clasped her fingers. 'Oh, Kasey, it's good to see you! It's been hell out there without you these past months.' His face flushed and he shook his head. 'I had to come—I needed to see you again. I've been sitting in the pub down the road since six trying to get up the courage to come in here. I felt so bad about the way we parted.' He swallowed. 'Hell, Kasey, don't look at me like that!'

The hand that held hers pulled her into his arms and he crushed her to him, his lips urgently finding hers.

His mouth tasted of beer and Kasey pulled back, her nose wrinkling. She'd dreamed of this moment for three whole months. Three long, miserable, lonely months. Since Greg had told her he had been getting engaged to Paula Wherry from Winterwood Station.

Quite honestly, when he'd told her about his engagement she'd thought he'd been joking and she'd laughingly refused to believe him. Paula was only eighteen years old, four years younger than Kasey, and as far as Kasey had been aware Greg had scarcely known the other girl.

Then Greg had explained. He was ambitious and one day he wanted to be boss of his own station. He couldn't do that working on Akoonah Downs, Kasey's father's property. Not that he didn't appreciate all Kasey's father had done for him, but he knew Akoonah Downs would eventually belong to Kasey's brother Peter, so there was no room on the Downs for him. Whereas Henry Wherry, who owned Winterwood Station, was seventy. He'd married late in life and Paula was his only daughter.

Kasey had been stricken. For as long as she could remember her life had been tied up with the tall, blond, blue-eyed Greg Parker. Hurt and bewildered, she had barely been able to believe her happiness had shattered into a thousand pieces.

The worst of it had been that she had had to keep her pain inside her, her pride not allowing her to show her family just how devastated she had been. Not to her father, not to Jessie, their housekeeper, who'd been the only mother she'd ever known. At least her brother and his wife and baby son were in the States, so she hadn't had to pretend to Peter that Greg's rejection hadn't mattered.

She'd known her father and Jessie had watched her warily, but she had covered her pain, made herself go on as before. Yet she had been aware that she wouldn't be able to continue under the strain of keeping up the pretence of careless happiness.

So she had run away to the city, telling her father she'd decided to take up the job offer she'd had months before. The mother of an old school friend ran a modelling agency, and she had always told Kasey that she would be perfect, with her height and looks.

Kasey stood five feet ten in her stockinged feet, and she knew her unusual colouring was striking—red hair and pale creamy skin, her rusty-brown eyes reflecting the colour of her hair.

'Oh, Kasey, you feel so good,' Greg murmured, his lips against her ear, his hands sliding beneath the waistband of her sweatshirt to move over the bare skin of her back.

'Greg.' Kasey leant gently against him.

'Just let me hold you, love. I've been thinking about this all these months. Why did you leave without saying goodbye?'

'Why did I...? How could I stay, Greg, after what you'd told me?'

'I guess—oh, hell, Kasey, I never meant for you to get hurt.' He raised pain-filled blue eyes. 'I know I shouldn't be here—everyone thinks I'm at the cattle sales—but I missed you like crazy. I had to see you.'

'Oh, Greg!' Kasey relaxed into his embrace. 'I missed you too. Hold me close.'

Greg's arms tightened and his lips urgently found hers again. Kasey returned his kiss with all the ardour of her three months of loneliness, of yearning for the familiarity of her family, and Greg.

The feeling intensified, passion rising, and from somewhere far off something was warning Kasey that she should defuse the emotive moment, but she refused to take heed. This was Greg, and she had loved him all her life.

How they got into the bedroom she couldn't remember, but the feel of the soft douna beneath her brought her back to some semblance of awareness of the situation. 'Greg—no, we can't...' she began shakily.

He slipped her sweatshirt upwards and his lips explored the soft creamy skin above the lace of her bra.

'You feel so good, Kasey. I knew you would. I've been dreaming of this for so long!' His fingers fumbled shakily for the clasp of her bra.

'I have too.' Kasey lifted herself and the offending garment broke free.

Greg's hand moulded her breast and he gazed up at her, eyes burning. 'Have you?'

'You know all I've ever wanted since I was eight years old was to marry you.' She smiled at him, her fingers twining in his fine blond hair.

His eyes flickered, fell from hers, and she felt a change in the tension of his body.

'Greg?' She frowned questioningly. 'What's wrong? You...you do love me, don't you?'

'You know I do. I always have.'

Kasey relaxed, her hand cupping his face. 'How long can you stay?' She paused, frowning slightly again. 'Why did you tell everyone you were going to the cattle sales? Surely——'

A cold numbness clutched at her as Greg's eyes slid from hers again.

'Greg?'

'Don't let's talk, Kasey,' he murmured softly. 'I want you so badly.' His lips moved over her breast and a shaft of desire flickered and then died as her mind grappled with the implications of the secrecy of his visit.

'Greg, what about...?' She swallowed, suddenly feeling decidedly nauseous. 'Are you and Paula...? You haven't broken your engagement to Paula, have you?' she got out, her eyes imploring him to deny her suspicions.

He made no comment, and the distant bleep of a car horn in the street below seemed deafening in the silence.

'Have you, Greg?' she repeated.

He moved negatively.

'But——' Kasey drew a quivering breath '—I don't understand.'

'Kasey, I can't not marry Paula,' he began.

She pulled her sweatshirt down over her nakedness, chilled with hurt and self-disgust. 'Then why are you here, Greg?' she choked out.

'Because I couldn't face not seeing you, not...'

She struggled away from him, off the bed, and crossed the small room to stand facing him accusingly.

Slowly he sat up, his elbows on his knees, his head in his hands.

'If you're still engaged to Paula...' Kasey wrapped her arms about her body. 'But you came here, we...we almost made love! Surely you can't mean to go through with the engagement?'

He looked up then, his eyes agonised, his lips as pale as his face. 'I never intended it to go this far, Kasey. I just—when I saw you, I just had to hold you. I didn't plan it, please believe that.'

Kasey had to prevent herself from flinching as though he'd physically struck her.

'I want you, Kasey, I can't deny that, but I can't let it make a difference. I've—well, I've made my decision about Paula and I have to stick by it.'

Numbed, she stood watching him. It was a nightmare—it had to be. This couldn't be happening!

'Forgive me, Kasey.' Greg stood up, made to come towards her, but she held up her hand as if to ward him off.

'What if we *had* made love?' she asked flatly.

He shook his head. 'Kasey——'

'You're still going to marry her?'

'At the end of November.'

She knew her tormented expression showed him her hurt and pain, but she was incapable of disguising it. His rejection cut her to the very depths of her soul, and in that moment even her pride couldn't rally to her defence.

Greg swung away from her. 'Kasey, I'm sorry. I shouldn't have come. I thought I could call on you, see you, and just... I was a bloody fool.' He took a couple of stiff, faltering steps, as though his legs were having trouble obeying him, then he drew a ragged breath. 'Kasey——?'

She turned from him, and interminable seconds later the outer door to the flat opened and then closed decisively behind him.

For long anguished moments Kasey stood where he'd left her, then nausea took hold and she ran for the bathroom. Afterwards she washed her pale face and stumbled back to the living-room, drained and yet surprisingly tearless.

She stood stiffly in the middle of the room. Surely she should be crying? But she was numb. Fourteen years of her life, her hopes had just been picked up, mended, and then smashed for the second time in three months. How could Greg have done that to her?

She supposed she'd fallen in love with him the moment she'd set eyes on him when she had been a shy eight-year-old and he had been a grown-up sixteen. Making him notice her had become the project of her young life.

Greg had turned up on Akoonah Downs, her father's cattle station, looking for a job. He had been the same age as Kasey's brother Peter, and their father had needed hands, so he had taken on the tall, blond-haired youth. Kasey had followed Greg and Peter around the station, riding, rounding up herds, checking fences, even repairing machinery, until she had been almost as proficient as the boys had been—much to Peter's disgust and her father's amused pride.

Greg and Peter had become firm friends, and Kasey's love for Greg had only grown as she had. Back then she'd thought her life had been all mapped out. She would marry Greg, they would live on Akoonah Downs and have lots of children. Happily ever after.

She sank into an easy chair. Greg had been her life. She had never noticed anyone else, even when she'd gone away to school.

Happily ever after. At seventeen it had been so easy.

Pain clutched suddenly at her, and recklessly she crossed to the small cabinet where her flatmate kept a bottle of Scotch someone had given them.

Kasey rarely drank anything alcoholic, apart from an occasional glass of wine with a meal, and she picked up the almost full bottle and gazed at it. Defiantly she fetched a tumbler and some ice and splashed in a measure of amber liquid.

She took a gulp of the fiery spirit and very nearly choked as it burned her throat, taking her breath away. Ugh, it was horrible! She wiped the tears from her eyes. Perhaps if she sipped it? But that was no better. She just couldn't drink the stuff. What a cheap drunk she'd turned out to be!

She blinked, feeling a little dizzy. Had that one mouthful made her feel light-headed? Hardly, she chided herself derisively. It seemed she couldn't even drink herself into oblivion.

She grimaced angrily and set the unfinished drink on the cabinet. She had already been sick once this evening, and forcing herself to get drunk wouldn't help, she realised that.

Then what could she do? She couldn't stay here; the four walls of the empty flat were crowding in on her. Before she had been conscious of the thought, she had taken her lined denim jacket from the cupboard by the door and had raced out into the street.

She walked for what seemed like hours, but when she eventually glanced at her wristwatch it was still only just after nine-thirty. She hadn't noticed her direction, but looking about her she saw that the street was familiar to her.

Of course. There on the corner was the hotel bar her flatmate had taken her to a few times with her group of friends. Cathy was away, but maybe some of the group would be there. Before she could change her mind she opened the door to the lounge and went inside.

The noise was loud but not deafening, and Kasey glanced around for a familiar face.

'Hi!' called a girl with long blonde hair.

Kasey recognised her—Anna, a cousin of her flat-mate's, and she pushed through the throng to the crowded table. A chair materialised and someone handed her a drink, which she sipped gratefully. With the din of the music and the conversation of the other seven people crushed around the table, Kasey didn't need to talk. It was enough that she could be distracted from her own pain-filled thoughts.

She took another sip of the drink, this time quite liking the sweetish taste of what was a popular wine cooler, a mixture of light wine and tropical fruit juice.

The noise was a cocoon, and after a while she began to be aware of herself again. Her eyes went to the drink in her hand. Was it the first one she'd had or the second? She couldn't remember. But it certainly tasted better than the Scotch.

She looked up at the people around her. Anna and her boyfriend. His brother and a dark-haired girl. The other couple she'd never met.

Her gaze moved on, met light blue eyes that were fixed on her, and her breath caught somewhere in her chest.

She had the feeling those cold eyes had been watching her for some time. She lowered her lashes and then, regaining some of her composure, raised them to take in the rest of the man sitting directly opposite her.

He was a stranger. Or was he? Did she know him? He looked vaguely familiar, but surely she would have remembered meeting someone so compellingly attractive, for he was certainly that.

His hair was black, short at the front and springing fashionably from his brow, and there were flecks of grey in the dark strands over his temples. His jaw was firm and square, and even though he was seated Kasey could tell he was tall. The loose folds of his grey bomber jacket couldn't disguise the breadth of his shoulders, and his pale aqua shirt was opened at the neck, showing a wedge of tanned throat and chest.

Her eyes rose to meet his gaze again, and she flushed when one dark, arrogant brow went up in silent query. He had been aware of her scrutiny and it obviously amused him.

Deliberately, Kasey returned to her contemplation of her drink. He probably thought she was flirting with him, leading him on. Well, he was in for a big disappointment! Let him think what he liked. She hadn't the energy or the inclination to swap small talk with him or anyone else.

She twisted her glass in her hands, watching the play of light on the frosty pink liquid. And Greg's face swam before her eyes, reminding her of his duplicity. How could he? He'd been everything to her. Her years of growing up had been shared with him. Only him. Even her first kiss.

She was swept on a tide of painful memories and the scene, the sounds of the tavern faded, carrying her back to Akoonah Downs, to her favourite spot, their swimming-hole...

Considering that large areas of their cattle property were expanses of dried grass and thirsty, stunted scrub, the spring-fed stream in the midst of tall, shady trees seemed in contrast to be a fanciful mirage. But it was real enough for those who knew of its existence.

She was there with Greg. They'd been swimming, and now sat on the flat rock over the water to dry off. The scene came back to taunt her.

'Did you enjoy the dance you and Peter went to last night?' she asked. Her father wouldn't let her go unless he attended the functions himself, much to Kasey's annoyance.

'The dance? Oh, it was OK,' Greg replied. 'Same as usual.'

Kasey wrapped her long, thin arms around her equally long, thin legs. It was her one disappointment in her teens that in being so tall she was also thin, with barely a figure to mention. Apart from having red hair, that was, red hair and eyes a distinctive shade of rusty brown that seemed to take some of the red tones from her hair, making her appear to have eyes and hair the same shade.

She had a long face, but without a pointed chin. Her chin was softly shaped and showed the faint indentation of a cleft. Her nose, lightly dusted with the dreaded freckles, was also small and in profile had a slight upward tilt. Dark lashes, not overly long, fringed her large eyes, and her lips turned up at the corners in an expression of mild amusement. Her father said she had a smiling mouth, just like her mother.

With her creamy skin, she was unaware that her colouring and features were a quite striking combination, one that was to see her in great demand as one of the Cable Agency's models, her success almost meteoric.

'How come you and Peter didn't come home last night?' she asked Greg as they reclined on the flat, rocky ledge.

'We'd had a few drinks, so we decided to stay in town.'

'Where did you stay? At the hotel?'

'Er—no. With friends.'

Kasey looked up at him, seeing a flush colour his neck, and a flash of revelation caught her in the stomach. 'Girlfriends?' she asked in a strangled voice.

'No, not really.'

Her eyes clouded and his gaze fell from hers.

'Don't go looking like that, Kasey! We stayed with the Carsons—you know, from the grocery store,' he told her gruffly.

The Carsons had a son of Peter and Greg's age, and four daughters, all older than Kasey. Not one of them had red hair.

'It was kind of them to put us up,' Greg added, and she nodded reluctantly.

'It's just that the Carson girls are all so—well, so——'

Greg burst out laughing. 'They are, aren't they? I think Peter has a soft spot for Jenny.'

'He's not going to marry her, is he?' Kasey asked, appalled.

'I can't see Peter settling down for years yet,' Greg reassured her, struggling to school his features. 'Peter likes playing the field too much.'

'What about you? Do you like that too?'

He shrugged. 'Sometimes.'

'Do you make love to these girls?'

'God, Kasey, you ask the most embarrassing questions!'

'Well, do you kiss them?'

'I refuse to answer that in case it's taken down and used against me.' He tried to turn her query into a joke, and she bit her lip and was unusually quiet for some moments.

'Greg, would you like to kiss me?' she asked at last, and his fair eyebrows rose towards the wave of almost dry blond hair that fell across his forehead.

'Kasey, a girl doesn't ask to be kissed,' he told her.

'Why not?'

'Because she doesn't. Not in words. Hasn't your— well, hasn't anyone told you all about that?'

'The facts of life?' She waved her hand dismissively. 'I know all about that. Who wouldn't, living on a station all their life? But I've never been kissed and I want to try it. I want you to do it, Greg, to be the first.'

'Kasey, I can't.' He shook his head. 'It doesn't work that way. You have to want to kiss someone because— well, because they're special. You don't just——'

'But you are special, Greg. You must know that.' And she leant forward, placed her hands on his shoulders and put her mouth to his.

His lips were cool, she remembered that much, and she realised now he must have been stunned into immobility. She'd wanted to be kissed by him for so long that the eventuality was something of an anticlimax. She distinctly recalled feeling a little let down somehow. But then, her technique could not be described as anything other than totally non-existent.

'Didn't you like it?' she asked him worriedly, and he reddened.

'I—Kasey, I don't know what to say, except that I don't think you should go around kissing guys when the mood takes you. It could be misconstrued.'

'The mood only takes me when I'm with you, so there's no need to worry.'

He muttered something under his breath.

'Can we do it again?' She moved towards him, and he drew back.

'Kasey, this is madness! Your father would skin me alive if he found out.'

'It could be our secret,' she told him softly, hearing the change in his tone and sensing instinctively his weakening.

This time he met her, his lips on hers now moving gently, his tongue teasing her mouth open, and she stiffened momentarily before sighing a surrender. This was more like the kiss of her dreams, and a funny feathery feeling fluttered in the pit of her stomach.

She wound her arms around his neck, her fingers sliding into the damp blond tendrils at his nape. Greg's hands slid around her now, and suddenly the timbre of his kiss changed.

He crushed her to him and she tensed, unable to quell a rising fear. Her breath caught in her throat and she pushed urgently against his shoulders. For panicky seconds she thought he was going to ignore her pleas for release, but he set her free, swinging aside from her, his shoulders heaving as he caught his breath.

After a time, an eternity, he turned back to face her. 'You see, Kasey? You can't play at grown-ups. Things can get out of hand. You have to realise that,' he said tiredly.

'I'm sorry,' she murmured through swollen lips. 'It wasn't that I didn't like it. It was just that you frightened me. I wasn't ready.' She swallowed, feeling chastened and out of her depth. 'I guess I'm not like the kind of girls you like to kiss, am I?'

His finger lifted her chin. 'Don't go thinking that, Kasey. You are my kind of girl, believe that. But you're rushing things. Wait until you're older.'

'But it takes so long to get older!' She sighed frustratedly.

Greg smiled faintly. 'Not so long, you'll see.' He stood up, putting out his hand and pulling her to her feet. 'We should be getting back. And Kasey, I think we'd best just forget this happened.'

Her eyes met his, telling him that that was impossible.

'Your father wouldn't like this, take it from me,' he assured her, 'so we'll put it on hold for a couple of years.' His fingers cupped her cheek, and she couldn't quite decide on the meaning of the expression in his blue eyes. 'From now on we go back to the way we were with each other before this afternoon happened. OK?' ...

Kasey had nodded, not knowing if she had been regretful or relieved. She'd been so naïve back then. She still was.

Greg had continued treating her like a younger sister, although at times she'd caught him watching her and she had glowed with happiness, quite content to let him decide on the pace of their relationship.

Relationship! What relationship? Kasey threw at herself scornfully. She'd gone unwillingly to the finishing school her father had insisted she attend, convinced that when she returned, all grown-up, Greg would have to admit his feelings for her and they would marry. Oh, yes, it had all seemed so easy.

For all she knew Greg had planned to marry Paula all along.

A lump grew in her throat and she swallowed painfully, unshed tears stinging her eyes. Just when she'd thought she had been coming to terms with Greg's rejection, he'd turned up and raked over the coals, fanned the flames of her misery. What a fool she'd been! Still was. She should have more pride than to sit here crying into her glass of wine. But the trouble was you couldn't turn love on and off when you wanted to.

She took a steadying breath, and as she became aware of her surroundings again her misty eyes met that same cold blue gaze across the table. Had he been watching her all the time? Seen her pain? She had the feeling he could look down into her very soul.

She made herself turn to the young man beside her and begin a conversation. But she was instinctively aware when the tall dark man opposite her pushed back his chair and weaved his way to the bar.

He *was* tall, as she knew he would be, and her gaze followed him. He was well over six feet and he carried himself with careless confidence.

When he returned to their table he carried two glasses and set one down in front of Kasey. She looked up at him, wishing she could refuse the drink, but she had no wish to start an altercation across the table. And she knew everyone watched them with interest.

She took a token sip of the drink and her eyes flew to him in surprise. The colourless, effervescent liquid was straight lemonade. Did he think she was drunk? Of all the presumptuous——!

'We're all off to check out that new disco in town,' Anna said, pushing back her chair. 'Everyone coming?'

A disco. Kasey was suddenly tired, and her agitated need for company had abated somewhat. Right now she just wanted the oblivion of sleep. She pushed herself to her feet, and was surprised when the room swung dizzily.

'You coming with us?' Anna asked her, her eyes flicking from Kasey to the stranger and back again.

'No, I won't tonight, thanks.' Kasey shook her head, then wished she hadn't. She sat down slowly and carefully. 'I'll just finish my drink and then go on home. Thanks anyway.'

'OK.' The others began filing out.

'How about you, Jodan?' someone asked.

'Not tonight. I'll see you all again.' The deep voice seemed to come from way above Kasey's head and she didn't look up as the others left. But she felt the long, tall body slide into the seat beside her.

'I'll take you home,' he said, his deep voice as seductive as the love-song playing on the jukebox.

'There's no need for that. I'm not drunk, you know.' Kasey looked at him then, and had to admit that in close-up he was no less attractive. A faint musky aftershave gently teased her nostrils, and she took another sip of her drink.

Lemonade. He hadn't even asked her if she wanted lemonade. She disliked the sweet taste. The waiter passed their table and she recklessly ordered a Scotch.

'Don't you think you've had enough?' he asked without expression.

'No, I don't,' Kasey replied. 'And I don't care for lemonade.'

She slid a sideways glance at him. His gaze seemed fixed on the half-full glass he was turning in his hand. That hand was strong and tanned with long tapering fingers, and the glitter of a plain gold wristwatch flashed from beneath the cuff of his jacket.

'I suppose now you'll go into that spiel about killing my brain cells and damaging my liver,' she tossed at him.

'No. Sounds like you know all about it already.'

Her drink came, and he forestalled her by paying for it before her fumbling fingers could find the change in her purse.

Kasey took a mouthful of the Scotch and coughed. Ugh! It still tasted dreadful. How could people drink the stuff?

'If it's sorrows you're drowning, I can vouch for the fact that they'll all be there to face tomorrow,' he told her.

Sorrows? He didn't know the half of it. How would he feel if his life had been shattered like hers? Men were all the same—selfish and cruel. And condescending, she added, not taking the slightest bit of notice of the quirk of conscience that told her she was generalising and being a trifle hard on the stranger with the so-attractive mouth. She stifled a giggle.

'That stuff,' he indicated the glass of Scotch, 'won't wash them away.'

'Yes—well, tonight I won't have to think about them, will I?' she said shortly, her anger resurfacing, and she made herself swallow more of her drink.

'Care to talk about it? It might help.'

Kasey gave a soft, bitter laugh. 'I doubt it. And I don't need a shoulder to cry on either.'

'What did he do? Forget to phone? Stand you up?'

Stand her up? Kasey felt a wave of pain clutch at her. If only that had been the extent of it! What would this arrogant, sophisticated stranger say if she told him the man she'd loved all her life had decided to marry someone else? A girl who was younger, plainer, almost insipid, but who came with a large, lucrative property as part of the deal—a dowry, if you like.

She turned and opened her mouth, ready to shout at him, but the room swam again and she closed her eyes.

What would be the use anyway? What could this stranger—anyone—do? No amount of talking would make it right. Greg had been quite prepared to use her body tonight, but in the morning he would have left her. He was still going to marry Paula.

And suddenly she realised she would be expected to attend the wedding. At the end of November, Greg had said. Weddings were big social occasions out there in the sparsely populated station country around Akoonah Downs. How would she be able to bear it? Everyone knew how she felt about Greg. There would be pitying glances. She cringed. How was she going to get through it?

If only she could turn up with a man on her arm. Not just any man. A husband! Yes—a husband! It would serve Greg right if she married someone else.

That would show everyone how little she cared. At least then she'd salvage some of her tattered pride.

'Tell me about it.' His deep, soft voice broke in on her thoughts. 'Maybe I *can* help.'

Kasey drew herself together. 'You can't. No one can. Unless you know someone who's looking for a wife.'

Had she actually said that? Or just thought it?

She looked at the man beside her. Their eyes met, rusty brown and light blue.

'As a matter of fact, I do,' he said evenly, holding her gaze. 'How about me?'

CHAPTER TWO

KASEY stirred and rolled over in the large bed. What was that dreadful hammering noise? She opened her eyes and then realised it was her head pounding. She felt dreadful.

Swallowing, she grimaced in self-disgust. Her mouth tasted like the inside of a camel's sandshoe. As she struggled to sit up her stomach growled emptily, complaining bitterly. Only then did she take stock of her surroundings, and she caught her breath in shock.

The large bed was not her own, and neither were the pale apricot satin sheets that half covered her near-naked body. Her fingers snatched the sheet up to her throat. She was wearing only her bikini pants.

Her eyes widened, surveying the room. Rich cream walls. Thick pile beige-coloured carpet. Light brown curtains. Expensive polished wood furniture.

Where was she? She drew her knees up in alarm. How had she got here? She fought for remembrance. At least she was alone.

Her wristwatch indicated that it was ten-thirty on Sunday, and the sunlight streaming through the window told her it was morning. The evening before was a complete blackout. She remembered that her flatmate was away. And she recalled that she'd decided not to go out. What had happened after that?

The knock on her door. Greg. Had Greg come to see her, or was that all part of some crazy, pain-filled nightmare?

Kasey rubbed her aching temples. No, Greg had been real. He had kissed her. They had ended up in her bedroom. Then he'd told her he still intended to marry Paula. Yes, she remembered now, and her heart twisted. Greg had left her.

But what had happened after that? Kasey fought to recall the hazy events. She'd gone out walking and——

The door off to her left opened suddenly and she jumped in fright, her fingers clutching desperately at the sheets. A man, a stranger, strode into the room, stopping when he noticed she was watching him with wide eyes.

He was tall, six feet three or four, Kasey estimated, and he was extremely attractive. A small part of her recognised that as her heartbeats thundered apprehensively in her chest.

'Ah!' His voice was deep and vibrant and totally masculine. 'Sleeping Beauty awakes.'

He folded his arms across his broad chest and raised one dark, amused eyebrow. His hair was damp and he'd obviously just stepped from the shower. He wore a short black towelling robe that displayed a substantial length of long, tanned, muscular legs, and Kasey suspected that that was the extent of his clothing. She shivered, and tensed even more.

'Who...? Where...?' she began, and swallowed convulsively as her tongue refused to work in her dry mouth.

'Who? Jodan Caine. Where?' He made a sweeping gesture with one arm. 'In my bedroom. Don't you remember, Katherine?'

'No.' She started to shake her head and flinched, the pounding behind her eyes reminding her of her splitting headache. 'How did I get here?'

He turned and disappeared through the same door, into an en suite bathroom, from what Kasey could see. She heard a tap run and then he was back, sitting himself on the side of the bed, holding out two capsules and a glass of water.

'For the headache,' he motioned, and mentioned the name of an innocuous analgesic.

Slowly Kasey held out her hand and took the tablets, washing them down with the water. She emptied the glass, realising she was thirsty. 'How did I get here?' she repeated, the cool drink giving her a burst of courage.

'Don't you remember?' he asked with amusement.

'If I did I'd hardly ask you, would I?' she threw at him, feeling stronger by the minute.

'I brought you here in a taxi,' he replied, 'from the hotel.'

The hotel. Kasey searched her memory. Yes, there had been a hotel—the one on Collins Street. And a group of her flatmate's friends had been there. They'd talked, and then the others had gone on to a disco. But not this man. Her memory gave up then as she strove to bring the evening before into focus.

She'd had a few drinks. Not that many, surely? Had this man got her drunk? She turned accusing eyes on him. 'Why didn't you take me home?'

He shrugged. 'My place was closer. And I was in something of a hurry.'

Why was he——? A deep dark blush rose over Kasey's cheeks as the implication behind his words occurred to her.

'You got me drunk and brought me here to——' She went to get up off the bed and, remembering her state of undress, sank just as quickly back beneath the covers. 'My God, you're despicable! That's tantamount to rape!'

Both dark eyebrows rose arrogantly. 'Rape—a pretty nasty word, Katherine. But I can't somehow see you being able to make the charge stick. The taxi driver will tell how you were begging me to take you to bed.'

'I didn't. I couldn't!' She gulped in mortification. 'I wouldn't have done that,' she finished, a note of entreaty entering her voice. How she wished she could remember...

He reached out a hand and cupped her cheek, the gentle brush of his fingers tingling coolly on her warm skin. 'Relax, Katherine,' he told her softly. 'I was in a hurry because I could see you were in a bad way—nauseous and dizzy.' His cool eyes held hers. 'Nothing happened last night. You passed out in the elevator on the way up here. It was a struggle to get you undressed and into bed, believe me.'

'Where...where did you sleep?'

A crooked smile lifted the corner of his mouth—a nice mouth, firm, full-lipped, Kasey noticed.

'Right there beside you,' he indicated with a slight movement of his head. 'And slept is the operative word, on my honour.'

She gazed across at him uncertainly.

'I promise you, Katherine, you were out like a light, and apart from that I have this——' he paused '—quirk, if you like. I'm afraid I do demand some small sign of response from a woman when I make love to her.'

And probably got it too. The thought sprang into her mind without warning and she rubbed her hand over her eyes. 'I just wish I could remember.' She met his gaze and the light blue eyes struck another hazy chord. He'd sat opposite her in the lounge bar and had watched her. And she'd thought then that she might have met him before. 'Are you sure that—well, that's all that happened?'

'Well, not quite all.' His eyes never wavered from hers. 'You did make me a promise, one I hope you're not going to renege on.'

'A promise?' Kasey nervously dampened her dry lips. 'What sort of promise?'

'To marry me.'

She blinked, dumbfounded. 'Marry you?' she repeated incredulously. 'But I don't even know you! Why would I——?' She stopped, another memory flashing into her mind. A man on her arm. Greg's wedding. She'd wanted to save her pride, appear at Greg's wedding with a man—a husband. You see, Greg Parker, I don't need you!

'You said you desperately needed a husband,' Jodan Caine told her evenly. 'And I agreed to oblige.'

'*I* asked *you* to marry me?' she gasped.

'I guess you did. And I agreed. So I suppose you could say we're engaged.'

Kasey shook her head. 'This is ridiculous! I can't believe I'd...you'd...'

'However, we didn't quite get around to why you wanted a husband,' he continued casually when she made no effort to carry on. 'I'm most intrigued. Are you pregnant?'

'Pregnant? Of course not!'

'I thought that might be the reason.'

'Well, it's not. A girl doesn't have to marry these days just because she's pregnant. I—well, I must have been depressed, from the alcohol or something,' Kasey floundered. 'Why else would I make such a suggestion? And, if it comes to that, why did you accept such a ridiculous proposal? Were you drunk too?'

He gave a laugh with a cynical edge to it. 'No. I wasn't quite sober, but I was far from drunk.'

'Then why?'

'Perhaps marriage would suit us both,' he said, and his tone was flat and even.

Kasey's eyes met his and fell away.

Jodan sighed. 'Maybe I was depressed too. I lead a busy life, my business interests keep me fairly well occupied, so I don't have much time to get to know the women I meet. That doesn't seem to stop some of them displaying an almost avaricious availability.' He grimaced self-derisively. 'However, I'm under no illusions as to their motivations. My main attraction is that I'd make a reasonable meal ticket. Being married would at least get them off my back.'

Kasey wondered sceptically if he really believed it was only his money women were after. Didn't he look in the mirror? 'How do you know I'm not looking for a meal ticket too?' she asked doubtingly.

A ghost of a smile shadowed his face. 'The daughter of Mike Beazleigh of Akoonah Downs wouldn't be needing a meal ticket, would she?'

'How do you know who I am? Did I tell you?'

He shook his head. 'I already knew. I'd asked someone some time ago, when I saw you at some charity "do". You were modelling.'

'Were we introduced?' Kasey tried to recall. She met so many people in her work, and she had to admit to not taking much notice of anyone or anything, she had been so miserable about Greg.

'Quite informally, yes. In a group of people.'

She shrugged. 'Well, I don't normally drink much, so there's no need for either of us to be held by some silly pledges made when we were under the weather.'

'As I said, it would suit me very well to be married just now.' Jodan shifted on the edge of the bed and Kasey's eyes went to his tanned thigh—firm, well-shaped and covered in fine dark hair. 'But you skilfully ignored my question,' he persisted. 'What about you, Katherine? Why do you have such a burning desire for marriage that you'd ask a virtual stranger to find you a husband? With your looks I'd hazard a guess that if you put it about you had marriage in mind there'd be a stampede for your lovely hand.'

'I told you—I was a little drunk.' Kasey's gaze slid to the window, and she slitted her eyes against the brightness of the light.

'And depressed. Alcoholic melancholia, wasn't it?' he mocked. 'Do you hand out marriage proposals every time you imbibe?'

'No, of course not! I rarely drink. In fact, I don't like the taste of the stuff. It was just——' Kasey's brain floundered around for some reasonable explanation. She wasn't going to tell this man the truth. The man I've loved for years is going to marry another girl, one with a more remunerative inheritance. She momentarily closed her eyes. No, her pride wouldn't allow her to admit that to this so-assured Jodan Caine.

'It was just?' he prompted maddeningly.

She shrugged angrily. 'Oh, for heaven's sake! Perhaps I was anxious about being an old maid or something. I'm nearly twenty-three years old and all my friends are married. My brother's married. Most of my workmates are married. Maybe I was just worried about me, about being left on the shelf.'

'I find the idea of your being left on the shelf extremely difficult to believe,' he said wryly. 'Even allowing for your reputation, Ice Maiden,' he added softly, and Kasey's gaze snapped to meet his in dismay.

'In the short time you've been on the scene you have gained something of a reputation, you know, in our circle,' he told her.

'That's ridiculous!' she spluttered.

'Is it?' His mouth twisted sardonically.

'Is that really what they... what everyone calls me?' Her chin went up, anger rising to flash in her eyes.

Jodan's own eyes remained on her face. 'I somehow thought you knew, that you played up to it.'

'No, I didn't know, and I wasn't playing up to anything.' Kasey seethed inside, flashes of the past months coming back to her—scenes she hadn't realised had filtered through her misery. She drew herself together. 'It seems I'm the last to know. But I can guess who coined the description and why.'

He raised his dark eyebrows.

'The perpetrator of such descriptive eloquence,' she bit out contemptuously, 'would no doubt have been male. Models appear to have gained some repute as fair game, easy pickings.' Her face set in the aloof lines Jodan had seen as she'd marched gracefully down the catwalk. 'And I proved to be the exception to the rule on any number of occasions. Perhaps I dented a few macho egos in the process.'

'Including mine,' he put in softly.

Quite suddenly and vividly she recalled an after-show party not long after she'd started at the modelling agency. He'd been there. Jodan Caine had attended the expensive show and someone *had* introduced them. And he'd asked her out. She remembered now why those cold, light blue eyes had sparked a flash of familiarity. He had undressed her with those eyes and she had flatly turned him down. A flush touched her cheeks and her lips parted. 'Including yours,' she agreed levelly.

A spontaneous smile just as suddenly lit his face. 'There's nothing wrong with your memory now. You did deal my ego quite a wallop,' he agreed drily, and their eyes met, locked, were held by some indefinable compulsion Kasey found it impossible to explain or understand. His devastating smile ignited a peculiar quickening in the vicinity of her heart, spreading a wave of heat to the pit of her stomach, and she broke their eye contact with an overwhelming rush of fearfulness.

'I don't sleep around,' she began defensively, her mouth dry again.

'Then I feel quite unsurpassedly flattered to have you taking advantage of my hospitality.' The corners of his mouth twitched, and Kasey's anger revived.

'I'm quite serious, Mr Caine. I presume you find that difficult to believe, what with every female making herself so readily available to you,' she mimicked, and he drew a sharp breath, his jaw lifting. 'No doubt in your circle virgins are in such short supply you wouldn't know one if you had one!'

His good humour had vanished now and she knew a chill of apprehension. 'And are you one, Miss Beazleigh—the last of this endangered species in captivity?'

Kasey blushed.

'Then perhaps you could offer to augment my tremendous lack of experience in this direction.' His hand took hold of the satin sheet and began to exert a downward pressure.

Kasey's fingers whitened at the knuckles. 'No,' she began. 'I didn't mean...I... Please don't!'

He released the sheet, but her relief was shortlived, for he loomed closer, making her draw back against the soft, plump pillows. He placed one hand on either side of her, his eyes moving slowly downwards from her mouth to the expanse of creamy skin of the shoulder that had escaped from beneath the sheet.

Kasey tried to cover it, but his hand held the silken material fast. Deliberately he lowered his head and his lips touched her skin, nibbled on the roundness of her shoulder, the curve of her neck, lingered there, moved to her hand clutching the sheet, his mouth tasting each finger one by one. Then his tongue-tip traced the line of her jaw.

Kasey's breath was caught in her chest and her heartbeats thundered as each muscle in her body tensed. He was going to kiss her lips. She should stop him. She wanted no man's kiss except Greg's. Yet an urgency took hold of her, a desire to feel this man's mouth on hers, and her eyelashes fluttered downwards, her need defeating her instinct to repel his advances at all cost.

The mattress sighed as his weight shifted, and she opened her eyes a fraction. He was gazing down at her, and was that a hint of cynical amusement playing around the mouth that had trailed fire over her tinder-dry emotions?

'Ah, Katherine, don't you know not to throw out such an inviting challenge to a man all fresh after a good night's rest?' he asked huskily. 'If I'd had no scruples you could very easily have lost that which designates you uniquely unfashionable.' His eyes were mere slits, glittering his regained humour.

'Why, you——!' Kasey struggled to get her hand free, only to realise the movement had dislodged the sheet to display one full, pink-tipped breast. Flushing, she recovered herself as he gave a soft laugh.

'Don't stand on modesty, my dear. You forget I saw your alluring body last night—and believe me, there's no reason to hide such beauty. I even like the freckle you have right about there.'

His finger settled softly on the sheet just under her left breast, and Kasey could have screamed in frustration, her anger intensifying, and the very worst part about it was that this whole situation was her own fault. If she hadn't been so stupid...

'All right, so you can prove you know every inch of me, but ogling a woman's naked body when she's unconscious is not exactly something to be proud of, is it?'

'Definitely not. In fact, I'm depending on you to keep the "unconscious" bit strictly between us. I have my reputation to consider, and apart from that I'd hate my mother to find out,' he finished with an exaggeratedly worried frown.

Kasey suspiciously scanned his expression, certain he was mocking her. His mother! Was he serious?

'Look, Katherine——'

'It's Kasey,' she put in acidly. 'Katherine Claire—K.C. Kasey. I only use Katherine professionally, so stop calling me that.'

'Sure—Kasey.' He appeared to savour the word, then sat back, his distance releasing just a little of the tension his nearness had created in her. 'Let's be serious. About this marriage—I like the idea, and, quite frankly, it would solve a sizeable amount of my problems. I'd appreciate it if you'd give it some consideration.'

A rush of conflicting thoughts cascaded over her, to settle on the small church in the nearest town to Akoonah downs and Winterwood, Paula Wherry's father's property. Paula walking down the short aisle with Greg, and Kasey standing with Jodan Caine beside her. It was a tempting scenario.

'But why choose me?' She plucked at the sheet, fighting her surrender.

'Why not? You have the background I'd want in a wife, you're from a socially acceptable family and your father is hardly a pauper, which indicates that you aren't a fortune-hunter. And you're a very attractive woman.' He pulled a wry face. 'But you don't need me to tell you that.'

Kasey flicked a glance at him. And he was hardly un-attractive himself, she had to admit.

'What do you say, Kasey?' he pressed her.

'Perhaps I will,' she began.

'"Perhaps" won't do,' he said firmly, and picked up her hand. 'Yes or no?'

'All right. Yes.' Was this really happening? Could she be agreeing to this—this crazy proposal?

'Good. Then we need a ring. Are you free tomorrow?'

'Tomorrow?' Kasey bit her lip. He was rushing her. 'There's plenty of time. We needn't——'

'On the contrary, my dear. When I make up my mind about something I see no reason for delay. We've decided to get married, so——' he frowned slightly and rubbed one tanned hand along his freshly shaven jaw '—say we make it next month? The sixteenth?' He regarded her levelly.

CHAPTER THREE

AT LEAST once a day during the next five weeks Kasey had lifted the receiver to telephone Jodan and call off their wedding. How, she asked herself for the hundredth time, had she allowed herself to get into this situation? Now, in less than twenty-four hours, she would become the wife of Jodan Caine.

She tossed restlessly in the unfamiliar bed in the suite her father had taken at one of the best hotels in the city. She wanted to weep, but she was somehow beyond tears.

She'd made a complete and utter mess of her life, a life she had only short months ago imagined was perfect. Then it had shattered into a thousand pieces, ending in this unbelievable nightmare.

Her childhood, she supposed, had been sheltered. She was unable to remember her mother, who had died when she had been just a toddler, so her world had revolved around her father, her older brother Peter, Jessie their housekeeper and, of course, Greg.

She had gone to the best girls' schools and colleges and mixed with the children of families considered to be the élite in Australia. Her education would be considered to be flawless, yet she was beginning to wonder if it had all been a total waste of time. Or perhaps she suffered from a disease that caused the abrupt cessation of emotional growth somewhere around twelve years old. She suspected she must have somehow gone around with her eyes closed all her life. Or perhaps she'd only allowed herself to see what she'd wanted to see, shutting out the unpalatable. Apart from her schooldays, her life had been rather isolated.

Her father was a true gentleman; she could recognise that now she had seen a little of the world herself. In fact, her father was so far removed from the norm in this alien outside world that it was almost laughable. Mike Beazleigh had been a cattleman like his father and his grandfather, and could ride and swear with the best of them. But not in front of Kasey. Her father still believed that a female needed a man's protection. She had had to do some rather smart talking to convince him that she would be fine sharing a flat in the city.

Kasey made a small sound, half-laugh, half-sigh of pain. She could imagine what would have happened to her here in the city had she not been so wrapped up in the misery caused by Greg's perfidy. No wonder they called her the Ice Maiden! In retrospect, she knew she had had no guidelines with respect to the male of the species, even though she'd grown up in a family of men.

Men. There had only been one man: Greg Parker. Her fair-haired knight in shining armour, who'd ridden up to Akoonah Downs and had stolen her heart.

Angrily she tried to shove thoughts of Greg from her mind. Her wedding eve was not the time to begin thinking about Greg.

The invitation to his wedding had arrived at her flat the week after Greg's surprise visit, and the embossed envelope had seemed to burn her fingers as she'd held it. 'Mr Henry Wherry requests the pleasure of the company of Miss Katherine Beazleigh and friend at the wedding of his only daughter, Paula, to Gregory Parker.' To be solemnised at the local church a month or so after Kasey's own wedding.

Miss Katherine Beazleigh and friend. Friend? Kasey could have laughed. By tomorrow night it would read Mr and Mrs Jodan Caine.

Jodan Caine—surely every woman's dream. Tall, dark, handsome. Part of a wealthy family, but also extremely successful in his own right.

John Caine, Jodan's father, liked to describe himself as a self-made man, and that was an apt enough depiction. He'd built Caine Electricals up from a small-scale electrical appliance repair business, housed in the back of a tin shed, into the multi-million-dollar concern it was today. The company's distinctive high-rise office block in the centre of the city was an attractive landmark, portraying undeniable affluence. In fact, John Caine had been a millionaire well before his marriage to Margaret Forsythe, the only daughter of one of the state's oldest and wealthiest families.

Thus, Jodan and his brother David, older than Jodan by four years, had been born with the proverbial silver spoons in their mouths. They too had gone to the best schools, mixed with the so-called best families, and a life of ease had stretched out before them both.

Yet John Caine hadn't allowed his sons into the family business before they had each served an apprenticeship of sorts. They had had to prove themselves by learning, virtually from the bottom up, every facet of Caine Electricals. Or so Kasey's father-in-law-to-be had told her, much to Jodan's wry amusement.

However, it seemed Jodan's interest had always been in computers, and when he was twenty-five he'd taken the legacy left to him in trust by his maternal grandparents, and with his father's blessing had branched out on his own in that field. With obviously outstanding success.

And now, ten years later, he had decided to marry Kasey Beazleigh—when he could have had his pick of the country's débutantes. And Kasey knew everyone envied her...

Pain twisted deep inside her, and it went deeper somehow than Greg's rejection. It had nothing to do with pride but rather a heavy disappointment, or so Kasey told herself.

In those hectic, almost surreal weeks after their engagement she'd come to like Jodan, his good looks, his dry humour. And she'd admired him as a person. He seemed to care about people. But it appeared he was just like all the rest, with his own selfish axe to grind.

Kasey swallowed a lump in her throat. How she wished she'd never attended that party, his parents' fortieth wedding anniversary, only two humbling weeks ago. That night had changed everything. If it hadn't, she might even be looking forward to her wedding day tomorrow— and all it meant. Mightn't she? To be Mrs Jodan Caine...

No! She still loved Greg. Nothing would change that.

Yet the events of that fateful evening had only proved yet again that men could not be trusted. She had just allowed Jodan's good looks to cause her to momentarily forget it. Still, that evening and its revelations haunted her...

The Caine family home in an élite harbourside suburb was filled with friends and relatives all gathered for the occasion. Coloured lights lit the beautifully landscaped gardens—yellows, blues, greens, reds, washing multi-coloured shadows on the immaculately clipped hedges and shrubs.

The weather was ideal. A cooling breeze had sprung up after a warm, humid day. Young people splashed in a pool built to complement a ferny rockery, while older people sat about in groups talking and laughing. A number of men congregated around the beer keg and music played pleasantly and unobtrusively in the background.

Jodan's mother, barely five feet tall and dark like he was, looked far too young to be in her sixty-first year and the mother of a handsome, six-foot-three son. She was elegant and very self-assured, and when Kasey had first met her she had seemed just a little daunting. However, Margaret Caine had quickly put Kasey at her ease, informing the younger girl that she couldn't have been happier with Jodan's choice of bride.

Lying in bed two weeks on, Kasey could almost smell the heady scents of the flowers and shrubs in the Caine garden, hear the laughter, the splashing in the pool, the murmur of voices. Snatches of conversation returned, playing through her mind like a film on rerun, the tension building towards the dreadful climax.

Kasey mingled with the Caines' friends and relatives, quite enjoying accepting the congratulations on her engagement, her eyes sliding repeatedly to the tall dark man she was to marry. And his eyes seemed to find hers just as often. Or so she imagined.

'Ah! So this is the lucky young lady to be marrying my nephew.' A short, plump woman had joined Kasey, her slightly misshapen fingers clutching a walking-stick. She shuffled to a nearby chair. 'Sit here by me and we'll have a chat.' She patted another seat and Kasey sank into it, the fitted black skirt of the dress she wore displaying her long legs to perfection.

'I'm Jodan's Aunt Grace.' The older woman smiled. 'His father's sister.'

Kasey relaxed, liking this woman who gave off an aura of 'no nonsense in kid gloves'.

'So you're taking on my nephew?' Her eyes twinkled.

'Yes, I guess I am. Or perhaps he's taking on me,' Kasey parried easily.

Grace Caine's gaze went to Kasey's red hair and she chuckled. 'Jolly good! I'm glad he chose someone with a little fire. Some of the simpering cotton-heads he's been out with would have bored him to death in no time—and I told him so.' She waved her stick for emphasis. 'Sometimes I despaired of him, I might tell you!'

Kasey's eyes followed Jodan as he stopped to talk to a group of people, his head turned in profile to her. His features were almost classical yet totally masculine, and she felt a sudden quickening in the pit of her stomach. He was a handsome man, no matter which way you looked at him.

'I'm sure Jodan can look after himself,' she said quickly, just as suddenly finding the thought of Jodan with other women quite inexplicably abhorrent.

'Oh, don't mind the women in his past, my dear.' Grace tapped Kasey's hand. 'Jodan's quite besotted by you, make no mistake about that. And he'll make you a wonderful husband.' Her eyes went to her nephew. 'I've always had a soft spot for Jodan. Everyone thought he was something of a daredevil when he was younger, but he was just high-spirited. The trouble was he was so different from his brother. David's the serious type, and that's quite admirable in its own way, but it was too much of a contrast to Jodan's adventurous nature. Got Jodan into a heap of trouble, I can tell you!' She chuckled again. 'But I'm pleased Jodan's chosen his partner well. I was worried he'd make another mistake...' She seemed to realise she was saying too much, and stopped. 'But enough of that, my dear. Tell me about yourself.'

Another mistake? So Jodan had been involved before. Married, for all Kasey knew. She tried to keep her mind on her conversation with Jodan's aunt, but she was almost glad when Margaret Caine came to get her sister-in-law and help her inside to the smorgasbord supper they were having.

No, Kasey convinced herself, Jodan hadn't been married. He would have told her if he had—wouldn't he?

Jodan materialised beside her then and she turned towards him. 'Have you been married before?' she blurted out, and he laughed easily.

'No. This will be my first time,' he said teasingly, his eyes alight with amusement, and she blushed at the innuendo bright in their blue depths. 'Have you?'

'Have I what?' she stammered, completely disconcerted.

'Been previously married?'

'Of course not!'

'Ah, I forgot. My virginal bride,' he said softly in her ear as he guided her in to supper, masculine possession in the arm he slid around her.

'Here's Dave and Desiree!' someone called, and Kasey had no premonition of what was to come. She was, at that moment, still breathless from the thoughts Jodan's teasing words had conjured in her mind's eye, of her body and Jodan's, of his lips moving over her bare skin, of his hands . . .

She forced herself to regain some composure. She hadn't as yet met David Caine and his wife, as they had been overseas for the past six weeks.

There were greetings called out and Jodan's mother embraced her elder son before putting her cheek to her daughter-in-law's.

David Caine could not have been less like his younger brother. He was a few inches shorter than Jodan and not nearly as broad. Jodan's Aunt Grace had told her David was the serious one, and Kasey recalled Jodan mentioning that his brother had hated the practical side of the family business, that David was management down to the last neatly brushed hair on his head. Jodan had said their father couldn't have been happier, knowing his elder son would step into his shoes when he handed over the business, referring to David as a chip off the old block.

And Kasey could see that David Caine was exactly that. He certainly looked the part. He was a younger replica of his father, while Jodan physically resembled his mother's family, with the Forsythe colouring and the tall rangy build of his maternal uncles. Yes, Jodan and David Caine were so dissimilar that an outsider would have been forgiven for disbelieving they were brothers.

Kasey shifted her scrutiny to David's wife, Desiree. She was, amazingly, smaller than Jodan's mother. Her white-blonde hair, shining in the light like spun silk, fell to her shoulders, turning under at the ends, giving her an ethereal beauty.

As she watched the other girl, Kasey quite suddenly became aware of a subtle change in Jodan. Imperceptibly, he had tensed. Had he not had his hand on her arm she probably wouldn't have noticed, and she shot a sideways glance at him.

His face bore no extreme expression—in fact it was almost studiously bland, but a slight pulse beat in his jaw and his eyes seemed to have narrowed warily. Then he was moving Kasey forward, across the room towards his brother.

Closer now, Kasey could see that David Caine looked tired and drawn and far older than his thirty-nine years. She returned her gaze to his wife. There was no disputing the fact that Desiree was quite beautiful. Her eyes were huge and violet, and beside her Kasey felt almost gargantuan.

'Kasey.' Jodan's fingers tightened on her arm. 'Meet my brother David, and his wife Desiree. And this is Kasey Beazleigh——' he paused and his arm slid around Kasey's waist to pull her close to him '—my wife-to-be.'

That same tension had him in its grip, and Kasey felt bewildered by the vibes surrounding her. Then David Caine had smilingly stepped forward to kiss her cheek, offering congratulations, welcoming her to the family.

Over his shoulder Kasey's eyes met cold violet ones, and there was no amity there. Desiree's lips had tightened, and now Kasey could see beneath the carefully and skilfully applied make-up the lines of boredom and dissatisfaction on the other girl's face.

'Isn't it great, Desiree?' David turned to his wife. 'And we thought Jodan was a confirmed bachelor!'

Desiree's shoulder lifted irritatedly as her husband put his arm around her. She shifted her gaze to her brother-in-law. 'I'm surprised to hear you've finally been snared,' she said, her husky voice in sharp contrast to her almost 'little girl' appearance.

Jodan's eyebrow rose, his expression bordering on contempt. 'You've got the wrong end of the stick, Desiree. I rather think I inveigled Kasey, didn't I, darling?'

His eyes softened as he gazed down at Kasey, and for one wild, bewitching second she persuaded herself into believing that he was actually in love with her, and a burning, searing heat coursed through her, accelerating her heartbeats and turning her legs to water. A dull flush coloured her cheeks.

'You've embarrassed the girl, Jodan.' Desiree smirked, her tone suggesting one could expect little more from a gauche schoolgirl.

Kasey drew herself together, deciding that on first acquaintance she didn't much like her future sister-in-law. She was being unreasonably rude, in Kasey's opinion. 'Not at all, Desiree. I really don't care who entrapped who; I'm just absolutely delighted that Jodan accepted my proposal of marriage.'

There was a moment's silence and then everyone began to laugh, teasing Jodan, asking him for verification of Kasey's story.

Jodan moved his lips against Kasey's cheek and his breath teased her earlobe, making her shiver. 'Would Kasey lie to you all?' he quipped. 'She went down on bended knee and promised to love, honour and obey.'

Kasey turned her head to make a retort, but before she could comment he had kissed her hard on the lips.

'Well, I exaggerate,' he added, holding her gaze. 'Obey's a touchy word in these days of feminist enlightenment. It was only to love and honour, so I decided two out of three wasn't bad.'

Then Margaret Caine stepped in, drawing them all towards the meal, defusing the tightening tension Kasey sensed between Jodan and Desiree.

As Kasey ate the beautifully prepared food and smiled as John and Margaret Caine cut into their huge anniversary cake, she reflected that David's wife was not really part of the celebrations. Everyone tried to include her, drew her into the family circle, but Desiree held herself apart with her whole mien, exuding an aura of affected boredom.

When she looked back, Kasey's memories of that meal seemed to focus on the tableau, all the more potent because it ran below the surface of the general play of the occasion. David Caine warily watched his wife as she repeatedly made teasingly snide jibes at her brother-in-law. And although on the surface Jodan bore her ill humour with well-mannered tolerance, Kasey sensed the unleashed anger that held him tense.

And still Kasey had no inkling of the truth. That revelation came later in the evening.

A few people had actually left, and Kasey was feeling a trifle jaded herself; making conversation with virtual strangers didn't come easily to her. She wandered through the double doors into the cooler air outside the house.

Some of the lights had been switched off, and only the patio remained subduedly lit. She strolled over to the balustrading and gazed down towards the pool area, most of which was in shadow, apart from two main lights reflecting on the water for safety's sake.

Sighing, she sat on the thick cement parapet, which was still warm from the sun. In the shadow thrown by a large potted croton, she was unaware that her black dress rendered her all but invisible. The flare of a lighter caught her attention, and she peered desultorily towards the brief flash. A tall figure drew on the freshly lit cigarette, and Kasey instinctively recognised Jodan. He was leaning against the thick bole of a lofty palm.

With a faint smile of pleasure she stood up, crossing the flagged patio and descending the steps to the path. A tenuous quiver of anticipatory excitement caught at her, a feeling she refused to allow herself to analyse too deeply. Her fingers felt the heavy sapphire and diamond ring on the third finger of her left hand, and her lips lifted in a spontaneous smile as she quickened her step.

'What the hell are you doing out here?' Jodan's voice cut into the night with low, furious intensity.

Kasey stopped dead, poised on one foot, her heart fluttering in fright. For one split second she thought his harsh question was aimed at herself, until she realised it was impossible for him to see her around the bush that stood between them.

'Looking for you, darling. What else?'

Kasey caught her breath at the sound of the low, husky reply. Jodan had been addressing Desiree.

He swore softly.

'Such language, Jodan! I could ask you what you're doing out here all alone as well, now couldn't I?'

Kasey stood transfixed, knowing she should make some move to join the other couple. Or flee.

'I was quietly enjoying the solitude,' Jodan replied. 'And I'd like to continue doing just that. Alone.'

'Don't be like that, darling!' Desiree pouted. 'I've scarcely set eyes on you all evening.'

'I've been around. It's called circulating,' he said with obvious sarcasm.

'Very admirable of you. I'm sure your mother was suitably impressed. You can always rely on the Caines to do the socially acceptable thing.'

'Your complex is showing, Desiree. Why not take it back to the house?'

'You're a bastard, Jodan Caine,' she hissed.

'Perhaps. But I meant it, Desiree. Go back inside before someone notices you're missing.'

'Before someone notices we're both missing, don't you mean?'

'All right. Before someone notices we're both missing.'

Desiree laughed, a low, sexy sound that chilled Kasey to the bone. Surely Jodan and Desiree...

'You're looking well.' Desiree's tone was lower, impossibly huskier.

'Thank you. You'll be pleased to hear I've never felt better. Now——'

'Oh, Jodan, let's not argue! It's been months since we've seen each other.'

'Desiree!'

'Your father's inside, extolling the expansion of Caine Computers again.' Desiree seemed to change her tack. 'But then, you always said you'd make a success of it, didn't you?'

Jodan was silent and Kasey tried to turn around, move away, but she seemed rooted to the spot.

'Do you ever think about us, Jodan? About what might have been?' The words were so softly spoken that Kasey had to strain to hear them, and then she wished she hadn't. Her senses numbed.

'That would be a pointless exercise, now wouldn't it?' Jodan said cuttingly. He must have crushed out his cigarette, for Kasey heard the flick of his lighter again.

'I think about you, Jodan. About us.'

'Desiree, that's enough! This isn't the time or place for this conversation.'

'Where and when?' she murmured. 'God, I've missed you over the years! You don't know how many times I've picked up the phone to call you. Jodan, I need you to hold me.'

'For heaven's sake, Desiree,' snapped Jodan. 'Are you mad?'

'Only for you. Jodan, please kiss me.'

'Desiree, you know I can't.'

'Why not? Oh, darling, we both want it.'

'Have you no scruples at all? You're my brother's wife!'

'David doesn't care about me.' The pout was back in her voice. 'I might as well not be there for all he notices. As long as I play the good little housewife and mother, that's all he wants.'

'Then think about your children, Desiree. You've got two young daughters——'

Was there a note of desperation in his voice? Kasey swallowed, aware of the clutching, intensifying pain in her chest.

'But I'm not cut out for motherhood. Oh, I love Shelley and Lisa, they're nice little kids; but I told you before we went away, I'm so bored with it all, Jodan.'

Jodan sighed. 'I can't help that, Desiree—and, as I've also told you, I don't fancy being a bored little housewife's diversion.'

'You don't mean that. Jodan, we could be discreet—no one need know. Oh, darling, I've never stopped loving you.'

There was a brief scuffle and Jodan swore again. 'Haven't you forgotten something, Desiree? In two weeks' time I'm going to be married.'

Desiree's laugh was low and mocking. 'Oh, yes. To the Ice Maiden.'

Kasey heard Jodan's swiftly drawn breath. Or was it her own?

'Why so surprised, Jodan? Don't you think I'm capable of making a few enquiries? And you forget, the Caine money opens society's doors to even little old low-class me.' Desiree laughed again. 'It wasn't so difficult. Everyone's talking about the match of the season—the moneyed Caines crossing with the moneyed Beazleighs.'

'Money has nothing to do with it, Desiree.'

'Says one who's never been without it,' Desiree put in with some bitterness. 'But I'm disappointed in you, Jodan, as far as your choice of a bride goes. Oh, she's attractive enough if you like redheads, but she's such an Amazon. Couple that with her Ice Maiden image and it will be like going to bed with a——'

'Desiree—cool it!' Jodan broke in angrily. 'I'm marrying Kasey, and you'd be well advised to get used to the idea.'

'Why, Jodan? Why are you really marrying her? I mean, it's all so sudden. You scarcely know her. By all accounts it can't be more than a couple of months at the outside.'

'Maybe it was love at first sight.' The bitterness in his voice cut Kasey to the quick.

'There was a time when you said that was how you felt about me, Jodan,' Desiree said softly.

'That was a long time ago, before I found out what a two-faced, mercenary little bitch you really were.'

'It's easy for you to judge me, isn't it? You never understood, Jodan. I needed security—financially, I mean. You weren't dragged up in poverty, otherwise you might be able to appreciate how I felt. David's future was set while you were just starting out. I couldn't take a chance on you. But I still love you, Jodan. I always will.'

'Love?' Jodan mocked her. 'You wouldn't know the meaning of the word. You disgust me, Desiree. Just get out of my sight! Go on back to your husband where you belong.'

'So self-righteous, aren't you? Well, I can wait.'

'Don't hold your breath, Desiree.'

'For as long as it takes,' she continued as though he hadn't spoken, 'because I know you still love me.'

'I don't love you,' Jodan said flatly, and Desiree snorted derisively.

'We belong together—we always did. And talking of love, Jodan, she's no more in love with you than you are with her.'

'I'm not discussing this with you, Desiree, so give it a rest and go inside.'

'Oh, I'm not saying she's not sexually attracted to you. She definitely wants your body, lover.' Desiree gave a throaty chuckle. 'I can't blame her for that. Don't we all? You always were the best in bed——'

'Desiree, I've never struck a woman in my life, but I'd say there's always a first time,' growled Jodan.

'I don't mind, tiger. Hit me if you want to.'

Jodan's silence was heavier than a blow.

'It's all show, isn't it, this marriage?' Desiree went on. 'You're marrying her as a smoke-screen in case everyone finds out you're still crazy about me, about your own brother's wife.'

'Desiree——'

'That's it, isn't it? I can hear it in your voice and I can see it in your eyes. You still want me, Jodan. Your body gives you away.' She gave that same low, sensual laugh. 'Well, I can be patient, lover, and I always get what I want. When you're tired of trying to thaw the Ice Maiden, you know where to find me. I'll be waiting.'

As Jodan moved, Kasey stepped hastily backwards into the shelter of a bush, not knowing how she had commanded her numb muscles to work. Then nausea rose inside her. The distinctive odour of Desiree's perfume assaulted her nostrils as the other girl flounced past her. She fought the rising dizziness, but it was some time before she could slowly follow the other couple up to the house...

* * *

It hadn't helped that Jodan had flown out the following Monday for Western Australia to handle some problem that had arisen in his new branch of Caine Computers in Perth. He hadn't returned until three days before their wedding.

By then the full realisation of Desiree's revelations had clustered, magnified and grown into a barrier stemming Kasey's usual openness. She had refused to examine the extent of her disappointment in her overestimation of Jodan's character. So she had remained silent.

Now, in a matter of hours, she would be marrying him. A man who had loved, who still wanted his brother's wife.

CHAPTER FOUR

AT SOME time in the early hours of the morning, the morning of her wedding day, Kasey fell into a fitful doze, only to wake up short hours later dazed and lethargic.

It took her all her will-power to drag herself out of bed to eat a breakfast she had to force down. As it was, she only swallowed a few mouthfuls of toast to please a fussing Jessie, who was all a-flutter, what with the wedding and the fact that she was in the hustle and bustle of a city she so distrusted.

Then after breakfast the morning seemed to accelerate as Kasey went to the hairdresser, collected bouquets, did the endless other small errands she could have delegated to someone else but knew she had to do herself to keep her sanity. She would have gone quietly to pieces if she'd had to sit in the apartment, waiting.

In good time she began dressing, donning the exquisite underwear, the 'something blue' garter over the sheerest of stockings, the 'something borrowed' lace handkerchief of Jessie's, slipping it into her dress, adding the 'something old' delicate heart-shaped locket that had been her mother's. And finally, the 'something new'— silver earrings which her father had had made to match the locket.

For her dress Kasey had insisted upon a simple, almost austere style in a rich ivory colour. It was an original from one of Sydney's exclusive bridal boutiques, and it could have been designed with Kasey's tall, slender body in mind. The dress fitted into her narrow waist, the skirt

cascading over her hips to swirl about her legs, whis-
pering sensually as she walked. The delicate, filmy veil
barely dimmed the red of her hair, and she knew she
looked her best.

Surprisingly, once she was dressed, standing before
the long mirror, she was quite calm. She could almost
have believed she was about to step out on to the catwalk.
Perhaps she was, and the rest was just a crazy nightmare.
She would wake up and it would all fade into the safety
of reality.

She even placidly dealt with a moment of distress when
the two little flower girls, Desiree's petite, blonde
daughters, succumbed to a bout of tearful nerves just
as they were about to climb into the limousine that would
carry them to the church.

In the car at last, she sat composedly, not really believing the time was now so near. Her hand betrayed not
a tremble as she lifted her bouquet, a mass of dark red
rose blooms and buds.

Her father was beside her, shifting on the wide seat,
fidgeting with the unaccustomed trappings of high collar
and bow-tie, flexing his shoulders and arms in his suit
coat. Irrelevantly she watched smilingly as he buttoned
and unbuttoned his jacket a dozen times before they
reached the massive spired church. She had decided to
be married in the city rather than face her friends and
neighbours at home in the country; in the serenity of
the familiar setting, the people, the places of her
childhood, she knew she could never have gone through
with this charade.

Then they were standing in the doorway, the long car-
peted aisle in front of them stretching towards the ornate
altar, the high, arched ceilings overhead, the faces turned
expectantly. But Kasey saw none of this.

There were two men at the end of the aisle, both dressed in immaculate pale grey suits. Her gaze flicked over David Caine's thinning hair to fix on the taller, darker of the two.

Jodan turned slightly as the organist played the first chords of the traditional Bridal March. His eyes, pale cold blue, met hers, and a bolt of pure shock at the enormity of what she was doing struck her, and rendered her motionless. Her step faltered, and her father put his hand over hers where it rested on his arm.

'Everything will be fine, love. Jodan's a good man,' he said softly, and she took solace and strength more from the familiar sound of his voice than his actual words.

The aisle seemed an eternity long as she moved, the two little flower girls following her one bridesmaid. Everyone had expected an entourage befitting the accepted appearance of what had been dubbed by the media a high society wedding, the merging of two of Australia's wealthy families, but Kasey had been firm about this at least. It had to be kept as simple as possible. She wanted only one bridesmaid, a girl who had been a friend from her schooldays, her flatmate Cathy Cable. And she had only acquiesced to having Jodan's nieces as part of the wedding party at the request of Jodan's mother.

As they reached the altar Jodan moved to stand beside her, and her quick involuntary glance took in the entire length of him.

To say he looked attractive would have been an understatement. His suit moulded his tall, muscular body, and the pale blue shade of his ruffle-fronted shirt was reflected in his light, bright eyes. In his lapel was a

deep red rose, matching those in her bouquet, and she
fancied she caught the heady scent of that single bloom.

Dearly beloved ...

The service, everyone told her later, was beautiful, but
Kasey scarcely heard it. She must have made the correct
responses, for it went without a hiccup.

I pronounce that they be man and wife together ...

Jodan lifted her veil and kissed her. And those brief
few seconds stayed vividly with her through the rest of
the ceremony. His kiss was a mere momentary touching
of his lips to hers, but the effect of that contact started
her shaking, so much so that she was barely able to sign
her name to the register. David, Jodan's best man, leant
over to laughingly pat her arm, telling her not to worry,
it wasn't the end of the world.

How she wished it had been! Or the beginning. If only
they'd met and fallen in love with no knowledge of what
went before for either of them.

She remained tense and trembly all through the seem-
ingly unending photo-taking session, the incessant flashes
of the media photographers. Somehow Jodan had arranged that the representatives of the press only appeared after the ceremony.

However, once at the reception she regained some of
her previous fatalistic calm. Perhaps the glass of something alcoholic Jodan pressed upon her had something
to do with that, although she made sure it was the only
spirituous drink she had during the evening.

And it wasn't until they reached the reception that
Kasey gave any thought to Greg Parker. With a shock
she realised she hadn't even noticed him at the church.
Yet he'd been there. At least, he and Paula were sitting
at the table with Kasey's brother Peter, who'd flown

home for her wedding before returning to the States to rejoin his wife and son on their holiday.

Greg looked pale and tired, while Paula leant close to him, darting adoring glances at him. Had she once looked up at Greg like that too? Kasey wondered, and suspected she had. But just at this moment it seemed light years ago, part of someone else's life.

Greg's eyes met hers and she swallowed at the raw pain in them, the taut angle of his jaw, and she was amazed that her only emotion seemed to be guilt.

She slid a sideways glance at Jodan, only to find him watching her through narrowed lids. Had he seen her looking at Greg? Would it matter if he had? He had no idea of her feelings for Greg, so he couldn't suspect— Kasey shut out the thought. Jodan would be the last person to cast aspersions at her. He had his own reasons for being here, for marrying someone he scarcely knew. She forced herself to smile tremulously, and make an inane comment about the floral arrangements on the tables.

The speeches were kept short and to a minimum. The meal, so they all said, was a gourmet's delight. Kasey couldn't recall tasting a mouthful.

Then came the bridal waltz, and she was swept into Jodan's arms. The panicky feeling returned. She was so very aware of his strong arms around her, his hands on her body. He had a husband's right to touch her now; she'd given him that only hours before.

She couldn't bring herself to look at him, but she could feel his gaze on her. Was he conscious of her wildly racing pulse, the thunderous pounding of her heart? Oh, yes, the experienced Jodan Caine would know.

Unable to stop herself she glanced up at him, and he made a soft sound in his throat, a sound that sent a shivery sensation suffusing her entire body.

'Ah, you've remembered I'm here.' He had moved her towards him to rest his cheek against hers. His lips were at her ear and his whispered words teased her oversensitive lobe.

Kasey drew back from him. 'I don't know what you mean.'

'No? I mean that's about the third time you've actually looked at me today.'

'That's ridiculous!'

'Is it, Kasey?' He gave a low, husky laugh. 'I should be thankful you at least checked it was me before you walked down the aisle. It would have been dreadful if the wrong man had been standing waiting for you, wouldn't it?'

Kasey's eyes flew to lock with his. What did he mean? Was he implying——? No, he couldn't know. She fought to regain some composure. 'Did you think I might have been expecting Tom Selleck?' she asked drily, with only the slight waver in her tone betraying the tension that held her.

Jodan grimaced. 'That pretty boy? Kasey, you can't be serious!'

Pretty boy? Perhaps. But no one could label Jodan Caine with that description. His features were far too strong, too masculine, all in all too vitally male. Jodan Caine was more compellingly attractive than any film star. And when she was with him Kasey had great difficulty bringing any other man into focus.

Even Greg. She repressed the urge to let her eyes move over the guests, to seek Greg out. Guilt took hold of her again. How could she forget Greg so quickly? She had loved him—still loved him. Didn't she? She glanced back at Jodan.

'You have the air of a princess waiting to see if I'll turn into a frog,' he said quizzically, and Kasey's movements faltered.

He dextrously readjusted their step. This was a fantasy, unreal. But the illusion suddenly became the only reality, and it was as though they were totally alone in a world of their own, the wedding guests fading into a shadowy distance.

'I won't, you know. I really am a brave prince come to whisk you away to my kingdom.' He swung her around, and Kasey's eyes shot to his face.

That was a mistake, for the amused quirk playing about his sensual mouth only added to his devastatingly dark good looks. Kasey felt decidedly light-headed and wished he hadn't twirled her about. That could only be the cause of her heady breathlessness. Yes, Jodan Caine was far too attractive for his own, or her own, good. The frog prince? He had to be joking!

'I'm sure you're the handsome frog in the lily pond,' she remarked wryly, and was rewarded by his deep throaty chuckle.

'I'll take that as a compliment, princess. You could have said toad.'

A tiny smile lifted the corners of Kasey's lips, and his eyes seemed to lock on them for immeasurable seconds before he spoke again.

'And happily ever after, Mrs Caine,' he said softly, so softly she barely caught the words. 'But talking of compliments,' he added, tense, waiting seconds later, his tone light again, 'you look divine, Mrs Caine. That dress is exquisite.'

The sheen of liquid sensuality shone in his eyes, and a faint flush rose to wash Kasey's cheeks. She felt hot and then cold, and totally confused.

'Thank you,' she replied, more than a little embarrassed. She had had countless compliments before, but none had the effect on her that Jodan's words evoked. He totally disconcerted her.

'All the same, I can't wait to see you out of it,' he murmured outrageously, and her blush deepened. 'There's a picture I have of you in my mind that's been driving me insane for the past five weeks. It haunts me day and night—especially at night. I see an expanse of smooth creamy skin, long, shapely legs, softly swelling hips——'

'Jodan!' Kasey attempted to curb his vivid description.

'Every beautiful inch of you,' he continued. 'And your hair, like cascades of fire flaring over the sheets.'

Something akin to fire began to spark, then spread in confusing abandon through her body. It was ludicrous, this whole thing, the ceremony, the reception, this waltz. She was allowing herself to be swept up in the romance of it all.

'Cascades of fire?' She raised her fine eyebrows. 'That's very poetic, Jodan,' she quipped, trying to lighten the oppressive conversation.

'You don't know how many times I've cursed my chivalrous streak, Mrs Caine,' he went on in that same sensual tone, 'for not taking advantage of you when I had the chance.'

'Had I been willing to let myself be taken advantage of, that is,' Kasey clarified quickly, and he laughed softly against her cheek, that same erotic arousing sound that seemed to strike traitorously some responsive part deep inside her to set her senses reeling.

'You would have been willing,' he said, and for all that his words were spoken softly, they held an arrogant assurance that rankled, and she unconsciously stiffened.

'Don't bank on it,' she got out between clenched teeth.

Their eyes locked, cold pale blue and rusty brown.

A small smile played at the corners of Jodan's mouth. 'I suppose it's history. We'll never know now, will we?' His gaze held hers. 'Until tonight,' he added, his soft words an exciting seduction.

Tonight—good God! What was she going to do when they were finally alone? Kasey's heartbeats faltered and then raced furiously. She couldn't imagine sharing the intimacies of lovemaking with a man she didn't love. How was she going to allow this man to...? All her adolescent fantasies had centred on being in love emotionally, and when her thoughts had touched on physically making love she'd always imagined it would be with Greg.

Now Jodan Caine, this virtual stranger, had every right to expect to kiss her, touch her, know her body as no other man had done. Not even Greg.

It should be Greg, a voice inside her cried, Greg she should be making love with tonight. But Greg would never be hers. And Jodan Caine was obviously expecting his wedding night to include a willing wife.

No, she couldn't! She'd have to somehow end this crazy farce. If she and Jodan made love tonight they would both be using each other as a substitute for someone else. There was no way Kasey could accept a physical relationship on those terms.

She opened her mouth to tell Jodan so, but before the words tumbled out her father had stepped forward to claim her, and Jodan bowed as he handed her over to the older man. But his cold blue eyes seemed to mock her, warn her that his time was coming, that she would be his.

Kasey shivered, and her father frowned down at her. 'What's up, love? Not cold, surely?'

She shook her head. 'No. Just... Oh, I'm a little tired, I guess. It's been a long day.'

And the long night stretched terrifyingly before her. Terrifying, yet inconceivably tempting.

The hours flew past as Kasey danced with her brother and other relatives, both hers and Jodan's. On the crowded dance floor she rarely saw Jodan as he part-nered the women guests. However, the swirl of people seemed to open up as he took his sister-in-law in his arms. Or so it appeared to Kasey.

Watching Jodan and Desiree as they danced, she had to admit they looked well together, Jodan tall and dark and Desiree petite and blonde. The other girl had the appearance of a fragile porcelain figurine, and to Kasey's eye Jodan held her in his arms as though she were every bit as frangible, as precious.

And they had eyes only for each other, Jodan's lips barely moving as he spoke to his partner. Desiree's hands slid around Jodan's neck, long, red-tipped fingers just resting on the tanned curve above his collar at the side of his neck.

Then Kasey's own partner swung her around so that the sight of Jodan and Desiree was lost to her view. She realised she had only seen them for mere seconds, yet time had seemed to stop, allowing the picture of the other couple to be printed indelibly in her memory. Coupled with that dull, undefinable ache of longing that was left to linger in the region of her heart.

'Kasey. Kasey?' Greg had to repeat her name before she realised he was standing by her side.

'Oh—Greg. I'm sorry, I must have been miles away.' She recovered herself as a tiny voice inside her mocked her. Not miles away. Just across the dance floor. In Jodan's arms. Blotting out the sight of the dainty figure who still claimed him.

'Dance with me?' Greg asked thickly, and Kasey's glance at him took in the taut lines of his jaw, the tired, strained look about his eyes. She softened and nodded.

Greg danced stiffly, with far less grace than Jodan, and Kasey had to concentrate on the steps, not allowing herself to dwell on making comparisons.

'It was a nice wedding,' Greg said, the words forced out between his teeth.

'Yes.' Kasey felt another spurt of guilt. But why should she feel any remorse? It was Greg's choice. 'How are plans for your wedding coming along?' she asked evenly, part of her wondering at her outward calm, her self-possession.

Greg shrugged. 'Fine. It's all being taken care of.' His eyes restlessly roamed the room, but Kasey knew he saw none of it. 'It won't be as grand as this. Paula's father hasn't been well, so Paula thought a big bash would be too much for him.' His gaze returned broodingly to Kasey. 'Are you coming?' He continued to watch her, his footsteps slowing as though he'd forgotten they were supposed to be dancing.

'Yes,' she replied hesitantly. She hadn't mentioned the invitation to Jodan as yet.

Greg's wedding. Wasn't that the whole reason behind this fiasco? Of course it was. That was why she'd married Jodan. 'Jodan and I will be there,' she added firmly, and Greg flinched.

'God, Kasey, this should be us,' he said thickly. 'Today—you in that dress, me in a monkey suit. It should be us, our wedding.'

'Greg, don't!'

'Well, it should. I should have... The other night in your flat, I should have made love to you then.' He stopped, his lips thinning tensely. 'God, I could tear him apart—the thought of him touching you!'

Kasey's eyes widened in surprise at the vehemence in his tone, and she shook her head. 'I don't understand you, Greg, I really don't. I thought I knew you like I know myself. But I don't. How can you——?' She shook her head again. 'The situation is of your making,' she finished with quiet bitterness.

His lips thinned again and he muttered an expletive under his breath. 'I just can't take this, Kasey. Seeing you in that dress, knowing you belong to that arrogant, upper-crust snob.'

'That's enough, Greg.'

'Why the hell did you have to pick someone like him, Kasey?'

She hardened her aching heart. 'Maybe I fell in love with him.'

Greg's eyes narrowed and he made a negating movement with his fair head. 'No. No, Kasey, I won't believe that. You're doing it to spite me, aren't you? To make me suffer. Holding him up as all I'm not.'

'Greg——'

'Money—that's what it's about, isn't it? And position. Well, I can't see your marriage lasting, Kasey. You won't be happy with his kind of marriage.'

'And what kind of marriage is that?' she asked icily, her anger smouldering.

Greg gave a cynical laugh. 'The high-class kind. It doesn't mean anything to his type, Kasey. He won't be the faithful one-woman guy you want. Women have probably been falling over him for years. Can you see him giving up that kind of lifestyle? In a few months you'll be wondering why he's late home from work.'

Kasey's legs felt like lead. Did Greg know how close he was coming to the mark? Only it wasn't women. Just one woman.

'You're not his type, Kasey,' he went on. 'You want forever. And you've sold yourself short on a womanising, high-priced playboy.'

'Aren't you presuming a little too much? I mean, maybe I've changed, Greg. Have you thought about that? Perhaps I'm looking for a modern marriage too.' She shrugged carelessly. 'The security of a wedding ring, but a loosely tied knot. I may want a blind eye turned myself.'

'No.' Greg shook his head. 'No, not you, Kasey. You wouldn't settle for that.' His eyes held hers. 'But he would. That's going to be your problem, Kasey—having to share him.'

A cold mask slipped over her pale face as she drew herself up, dropping a wall of icy disdain between herself and Greg. 'I think it's time I changed,' she said flatly. 'And I see Paula over there fretting for you. Goodbye, Greg.' She walked away from him, sick at heart, knowing she was severing ties with the whole of the life that had gone before, with her childhood fantasies, her secure fairy-tale imaginings. And with Greg.

'Don't you look a picture?' Jessie sighed, and wiped a tear from her weathered cheeks.

Kasey glanced in the mirror as she smoothed the three-quarter-length jacket of her suit over her hips and adjusted the complementary-toned shawl scarf she'd knotted carelessly around her neck to fall loosely over one shoulder.

Her going-away outfit was a gift from her employer, her bridesmaid's mother, and the cut had it fitting Kasey to perfection, the colour highlighting the rusty burnish of her mass of soft, naturally curling hair that tumbled softly to her shoulders.

But the face reflected in the mirror could have been a stranger's. The large cinnamon-brown eyes were the same. The high cheekbones, the sweeping line of her jaw were familiar. The wide red mouth was hers. But it didn't seem to be her. It couldn't be her.

It wasn't. Katherine Claire Beazleigh was no more. Today she had married Jodan Forsythe Caine, for better, or for worse. Kasey shivered. Katherine Claire Caine—such alliteration! She swallowed a hysterical giggle.

Her wedding day, a day washed in unreality, staccato fragments of conflicting impressions and thoughts, sometimes flashing past and then dragging along on leaden feet, wasn't quite over yet. She still had to play her part, keep a bride's happy radiance pasted on to her pale face.

'Oh, Kasey.' Jessie wrapped her thin arms around the younger girl, 'if only your mother could see you now! She'd be that proud.'

Kasey hugged Jessie back, loath to let her go, to sever what seemed to be her last fragile grip on the safety and security she'd known for twenty-two years. Tears welled in her eyes and she fought them back.

'He's a fine stamp of a man, that husband of yours, love.' Jessie's eyes were also suspiciously bright. 'You're a lucky girl.'

'Am I?' Kasey's gaze fell from the older woman's. 'I suppose I am.' But perhaps Jodan's good looks were deceiving. Greg's words echoed inside her: a womanising, high-priced playboy.

'There's many a woman who'd give her eye-teeth to be married to a man like Jodan.' Jessie patted Kasey's arm.

'I know.' The words were out, tonelessly, before Kasey could stop them. Of course she was aware of Jodan's attraction. She could almost allow herself to be swayed by it herself. And, in the short time she'd known him, she'd seen the looks women seemed compelled to give him everywhere they went. Even his own sister-in-law... Kasey bit her lip as Jessie continued.

'When you rang and told us you were getting married, I was worried you were making a decision too hastily, on the rebound from Greg.'

'Jessie, that's——'

'Yes, love, I know.' Jessie held up her hand. 'It was ridiculous. Greg was all part of a passing childhood fancy. When you spread your wings and met Jodan, you realised that the real thing is vastly different from an adolescent crush. And now I've met your Jodan too—well, I just know it's right.'

Kasey closed her suddenly slack mouth.

'There's no comparison, is there, love? Jodan's everything Greg could never be.'

'Well, I... Jodan...' Kasey felt another flicker of guilt as Jessie almost quoted Greg—'holding him up as all I'm not'. She drew a shaky breath. 'Jodan's very self-possessed and——'

'Downright sexy!' Jessie chuckled. 'Don't worry, I'm not blind to the pleasures of looking at a real man, you know. But it's not just looks, love. Greg's still got a lot of growing up to do, while Jodan—well, what can I say?' She chuckled. 'Jodan is what I'd call a real hunk. Plain and simple.'

Jessie was right about that, Kasey reluctantly acknowledged to herself. Jodan Caine was all man— physically. She shivered and made herself think about Greg. But somehow she couldn't get his face into focus, only managing a hazy image, one that was quickly supplanted by another strong-featured face with cold blue eyes and a bold, sensual mouth.

But it wasn't fair to compare the two men. They came from different worlds, their backgrounds poles apart. Jodan had had everything from the moment he was born, while Greg had had to make his own way on his own.

Jodan went out on his own too, reminded an inner voice, and he made more than a success of his project. And he hadn't had to marry the boss's daughter to do it.

'Jodan will look after you.'

Kasey blinked as she tuned in to the end of Jessie's reassurances, but before she could make any comment there was a knock on the door and Desiree Caine stepped daintily into the room.

'All dressed?' As she stood there, still holding the door open, her sharp violet eyes dissected Kasey's outfit.

Jessie made a muffled sound beside Kasey, something like a muttered 'Humf!' The older woman made no secret of the fact that she didn't care for Kasey's sister-in-law.

'You should be going, love,' Jessie put in. 'Jodan will be waiting.'

'He's not finished changing,' Desiree stated. 'I've sent the girls out with David, and Jodan asked me to see how things were going with the bride.'

'I'm just about ready.' Kasey's tongue felt too large in her mouth when she tried to speak.

'Don't let me keep you, Jessie,' Desiree waved a thin arm dismissingly towards the open door. 'I'll help Kasey finish off. We'll see you back out in the reception-room.'

There was a silent battle of wills for a moment before Jessie moved reluctantly forward, her eyes as they met Kasey's speaking volumes.

When the door closed behind Jessie, Desiree turned and leaned back against it, folding her arms as she faced Kasey. 'So, it all went off magnificently, didn't it?' she remarked. 'There's no substitute for sound financial backing, is there? No matter how short of notice the wedding was.' Violet eyes fell to the flatness of Kasey's stomach with less than subtle implication. 'We rather expected to see a shotgun under your father's arm as he led you down the aisle.'

'Then you must have been disappointed,' Kasey parried coldly.

The other girl shrugged. 'Time will tell all. It is one way to snare the prize, though.'

'Not my way,' Kasey bit out with ominous quietness.

'To each his own, as they say.' Desiree bit her lip. 'And who can blame anyone for wondering? There's no denying it was a short engagement.'

Kasey felt the conversation was heading on to rather thin ice. 'Jodan saw no point in waiting.'

With a flick of her curtain of silky hair, Desiree laughed softly. 'Jodan wouldn't. In fact, he's rather like a steamroller when he decides upon a course. Very macho!'

'If I hadn't wanted to marry him I wouldn't have let him steamroller me into anything.' Kasey mouthed the words and wished she could believe them.

'I'm sure you wouldn't. But he's a handsome devil, isn't he? Money, looks, sex appeal—Jodan's got it all. He always was one of the sexiest men around.' Desiree paused for effect and Kasey tensed, subconsciously waiting for the crunch, wondering why she didn't just cut the other girl short and leave her. But it was as though she was mesmerised, being pulled slowly into Desiree's sticky web.

'Of course, Jodan and I go way back,' Desiree continued, 'to before I met David.'

'I know,' Kasey told her flatly, and was rewarded by the flicker of surprise in the other girl's eyes.

'Oh.' Desiree recovered quickly. 'I guess it's no secret. I actually knew Jodan well before I met David. Jodan and I were——' she paused '—quite good friends in the old days.'

'I'm sure you were.' Kasey felt her temper rising at the innuendoes in the other girl's tone.

'Yes, Jodan and I were inseparable.' Her violet eyes met Kasey's, but Kasey ensured that Desiree's were the first to fall.

'But you chose to marry David,' she reminded her sister-in-law evenly.

'Yes.' Desiree moved away from the door, swaying across to finger the fine finish on Kasey's suitcase that lay open on the bed. 'David's a wonderful father to the girls, but he's hardly the most exciting of husbands.'

Kasey shifted irritatedly, tired of Desiree's cat-and-mouse game. 'I think I should be going,' she began as she closed her suitcase, slipping the catch with a concluding click.

'This sham of a marriage,' Desiree said matter-of-factly, in much the tone she would have used to comment on the weather. 'It won't last.' She struck a bored pose. 'Jodan's hardly been a faithful one-woman man.'

Kasey stiffened. This was the second time in less than an hour that her marriage had been doomed to the divorce court, Jodan's character painted in the worst of hues—by Greg, and now by Desiree. And the worst part about it was that, deep down, Kasey knew she believed it, too.

She'd have to be a naïve fool to deny that Jodan was far from being inexperienced when it came to the female sex. She knew his name had been linked with any number of women—everyone had been quick to tell her that. Even her friend Cathy had gently warned her about Jodan's reputation. And hadn't she herself thought about a divorce even before she had been married? she reminded herself guiltily. Yet her anger bubbled inside her, seeking escape.

How dared Desiree brazenly face her, sharing her sordid confidences, with Kasey's marriage to Jodan only hours old?

'Firstly, Desiree, my marriage to Jodan is scarcely a sham, and secondly, as to Jodan's experience—well, that's all to the good, you'd be the first to admit. Who would want a husband who didn't know where it was all at? I'm sure you get my drift.'

'My, my! She has claws!' Desiree's spiteful smile never went anywhere near her eyes. 'Perhaps I've underestimated you, Kasey.'

'I promise you you have.' Kasey's chin rose. 'And while we're on this distasteful subject which you insisted we discuss, I can assure you I'm more than enough woman for Jodan to handle. Do I make myself clear?'

'As crystal.'

Kasey's breathing was shallow and the fingers that clutched her handbag were stiff with tension.

'Maybe I should put my cards on the table too,' Desiree continued. 'Jodan's mine—he always was and he always will be. So you'll have to get used to that fact. When I crook my finger he'll come running back so fast it will make your head spin. Do *I* make *myself* clear?'

This couldn't be happening. Kasey's stomach churned sickeningly as she heard herself laugh lightly. Was she really doing battle for the possession of a man she didn't love, didn't even know very well? It had to be a joke.

'I'm sorry, Desiree, but I can't take all this seriously. You sound—well, to be honest, we both sound like the poor script from a second-rate, low-budget movie.'

The other girl's eyes flashed. 'You can be amused now, Kasey, but we'll see who has the last laugh. I still have a few aces up my sleeve. Jodan loves me, I tell you.'

'Then why didn't he marry you?' Kasey asked quietly, suddenly weary of the whole scene.

'Because he knew how much David loved me and he didn't want to hurt his brother.' Desiree's voice caught a little. 'It's been torture over the years, trying to deny our feelings. But sometimes—well, we're only human after all, Jodan and I.' She sighed expressively. 'Of course, David would be devastated if he knew, and neither of us want to upset him. He hasn't been well lately, and you know how people talk. So, in case some of the gossip reached David's ears, Jodan decided to remedy the situation. By marrying someone else. Anyone.'

Kasey bit off an angry exclamation and the other girl's eyes flashed brightly.

'It's true, my dear,' she continued. 'Jodan needed a smoke-screen for a while, until we sort things out. So he married you, to cover up our affair.'

'A somewhat drastic measure, wouldn't you say?' Kasey remarked sarcastically.

'But a fact, nevertheless.' Desiree eyed her reflection in the mirror. 'Jodan always comes back to me.'

'Not this time.' At that moment Kasey really wanted to believe it, to feel confident that Jodan loved her, that she had no need to fear Desiree or any other woman. But was it simply to deny Desiree the pleasure, or purely for herself?

'Oh, come now, Kasey.' Desiree snickered scornfully. 'I'll admit you do have a certain obvious charm——' her eyes flicked up to take in Kasey's mass of red hair and then fell to the rise of her breasts '——but can you honestly see a man like Jodan preferring your somewhat ample proportions to me?'

'Do you know, Desiree, I've always abhorred the word "bitch" when it's used towards any member of my sex, but you are, quite frankly, the meaning of that off-colour term personified.'

'And I really couldn't care less what you or anyone else call me.' Desiree sauntered to the door. 'I always get what I want, so just remember what I said, Kasey. Jodan's mine. I give him a month or so to tire of your greener pastures, then he'll be back to me.'

Ensuring she had the last word, Desiree stepped through the doorway, closing the door firmly behind her.

CHAPTER FIVE

JODAN'S hands moved competently on the steering-wheel of the comfortable BMW, the car's wipers throwing the film of water from the windscreen. After a perfectly sunny day, light rain had now begun to fall, growing heavier as they drove out of the city and headed towards the Blue Mountains.

Kasey sat in a numbed silence, her own hands lying limply in her lap.

'Are you cold?' His deep voice startled her.

'No, not really. It's raining,' she added absently, and he gave a soft laugh.

'So it is,' he said drily. 'At least we can be thankful the weather held out for the wedding. We didn't get the thunderstorms that were predicted.'

'I suppose so.' Did it matter? she asked herself wearily.

Jodan shot a quick glance at her before returning his attention to the wet black road. One strong hand left the wheel and felt for her hand, his fingers threading through hers, lifting her hand to hold it on his thigh. 'You sound exhausted. It's been quite a day, hasn't it?'

'Yes.' Jodan didn't know the half of it. And there was still the night to come.

'Would you rather we stopped at a motel instead of driving on to the house?'

'Oh, no, I'm fine,' she reassured him hurriedly, her mind throwing up a picture of a small motel room and one large bed. 'It's not that far, is it?'

'Not really.' Jodan glanced at his wristwatch. 'About three-quarters of an hour in this weather.'

Kasey tried to stir herself, making herself watch the dark, wet scenery, what she could see of it. Shapes of trees, a mass of shiny black leaves, bright windows in occasional houses, other headlights reflected glaringly on the black ribbon of road.

But her eyes kept coming back to the dimly lit interior of the car, to Jodan's hand on the wheel. And, if she shifted her head just slightly, the sight of their hands, his and hers, fingers interlaced, resting familiarly on his hard-muscled thigh. Her fingers curled instinctively and Jodan's tightened. Too cold? Kasey was suddenly far too warm.

'You said the house belongs to your family.' She forced herself to make easy conversation. Anything to keep her mind off the touch of his fingers on hers, a small intimacy presaging other intimacies to come.

'Mmm. Dad had it built a few years ago, as a retreat, I suppose. My mother loves the Blue Mountains and they spend quite a bit of the year there—gets Dad away from the pressures of the business. Have you seen much of this area?'

Kasey shook her head. 'No. We tended to go to the sea when we were away from Akoonah Downs. After station country the beach is like some kind of paradise.'

'I can believe that. It probably works in reverse for us. Living in the city makes the mountains Utopia. The view up here is breathtaking. The house sits on top of a perpendicular cliff about two hundred and fifty metres high. It's magnificent!'

Kasey shivered, and Jodan squeezed her hand again.

'There's something awe-inspiring about these mountains. I've seen some that are higher in other parts of

the world, but for sheer majesty the distinctive rock for-
mations, the colours of the trees, the blue tinge in the
clear air—it's fantastic. We don't give our natural
wonders due respect here in Australia.'

'You sound as though you love it too,' Kasey murmured, and his tone when he replied held a smile.

'I do. I decided quite a while ago that when the time
came it would be an ideal place for a honeymoon. No
neighbours to speak of, high up in the clouds. "A jug
of wine, a loaf of bread—and thou." And our part of
the Blue Mountains is just perfect as a stand-in for the
wilderness.'

Alone with Jodan Caine. Her heart raced. 'How far
is the nearest neighbour?' Kasey asked evenly.

'About half a kilometre.' He glanced at her again. 'You
don't mind that I've arranged for the Jensens, the couple
who caretake the house, to have a few days' break with
their daughter in town?'

Kasey shook her head. Normal honeymooners would
want to be alone. She swallowed, her mouth dry. Perhaps
it would have been better to have had the other couple
there. Surely Jodan wouldn't make a scene with the
Jensens within hearing? Now, alone in the house, how
would he react when she told him what she felt must be
said? That she couldn't go through with this marriage,
couldn't let him . . . He couldn't expect it of her.

But he could—she tortured herself with the reality of
what she'd done. She stiffened with apprehension and
pulled her hand from his.

They were winding along twisting roads now and
Jodan made no move to recapture her hand, as he con-
centrated on driving through the steady rainfall. They
had passed through a couple of townships, and before

long Jodan took an unsignposted access road off to the left.

'Not far now,' he said easily, and Kasey's heartbeats accelerated agitatedly. How she wished she could close her eyes, to open them to the hot, familiar dryness of the homestead hundreds of miles away on Akoonah Downs.

The gates were closed, huge white wrought-iron gates in a high-hedged fence. At eye-level on one gate was a plaque embossed with one word: CAINE. Jodan flicked a button on the remote control on the dashboard and the barrier swung smoothly open. The road wound still higher until it suddenly levelled out to display their destination.

The house was highlighted by unobtrusive exterior lighting that accentuated the planes and angles of its split-level design. That it had been professionally architected to fit the landscape, taking advantage of the natural contours of the land, was obvious, and the high-pitched rooflines gave the house its own magnificence.

Jodan drove the BMW under the roofed patio in front of the main entry and switched off the ignition. Light drizzly rain still fell, but the opaque roof protected them while the house took the main brunt of the wind. Jodan climbed from the car and strode around to open Kasey's door.

'Welcome to Valley View, Mrs Caine.' He smiled as he helped her from the car.

Kasey gazed around her at the leafy greenery of what she could see of the garden, and at the house, as Jodan climbed the few steps to insert a key in the door. He stood waiting for her to join him. She did so on leaden feet.

'It's a beautiful house,' she began, and before she knew what he was about he had swept her into his arms. 'Jodan, put me down! I'm too heavy,' she protested.

'Rubbish!' He stepped easily inside. 'It's traditional, carrying the bride over the threshold.' He kissed her quickly and let her legs slide downwards until they touched the floor. With his arm still around her waist he flicked on the light switch, bathing them in light.

His eyes looked dark as he turned back to her, his lips twisting in a crooked smile. 'I'm glad we decided to continue on to the house,' he said huskily. 'Go on in and I'll get our cases.' He turned and left her.

Bewilderedly, Kasey watched the retreating breadth of his back as he returned to the car. She'd just been lifted in strong arms and carried effortlessly through the doorway, all five feet ten inches of her, as though she were a featherweight. She could still feel the sinewy strength in the arms that had held her, and she shivered, her stomach quivering inexplicably.

Traditional. The whole day had been traditional. A traditional masquerade.

She watched Jodan's dark head as he bent over the boot of the car and drew out their cases, and a sudden tightness caught her in the chest. She wished again that today had been reality, a genuine commitment of two people, herself and Jodan, who loved each other, rather than this fraudulent facsimile she had allowed herself to be part of.

Jodan rejoined her, closing the door behind him with his foot. The subdued click of the well-oiled latch seemed to echo inside Kasey like the resonant knell of a portentous bell.

'I'll show you through.' Carrying the cases, Jodan skirted the half-dozen shallow steps leading down into the sunken lounge and crossed to a small flight of stairs to a hallway on the right.

Tentatively Kasey followed, her high heels beating a treble-toned tattoo on the cream Italian floor tiles. They passed four bedrooms until they reached the room at the end of the hallway, on the opposite side of the house to the entry. With a heavy sense of foreboding, Kasey stepped inside.

The walls were eggshell-blue and the huge king-sized bed bore a blue broderie anglaise spread. Teal-blue curtains were drawn across what must have been a wall of glass overlooking the valley below.

But Jodan had set down the cases and turned to face her.

If he touches me now, Kasey told herself, I'll scream hysterically!

Jodan raised one dark eyebrow and the corners of his mouth quirked. 'You look all in. The bathroom's through there,' he indicated.

Kasey swallowed, clenching her teeth to stop them chattering.

'I'll go and make us some coffee, while you freshen up. Unless you'd prefer something stronger.' Amusement brightened his eyes.

'No. No, coffee would be fine,' she replied through stiff lips, valiantly maintaining her dignity.

He'd expected her to jump at the chance of a drink, his expression told her that. Did he think she was an alcoholic? After one night of over-indulgence?

'Have a shower if you like, and then come on down to the lounge when you're ready,' he said easily, and left her.

Kasey slowly expelled the breath she hadn't known she'd been holding. Her chest felt sore and her body ached all over from the effort of a day of behaving correctly, keeping her expression bride-like. The strain of it all was finally hitting her.

If only she could just fall into the comfort of the big bed and sleep, drift away in peaceful, painless oblivion. She eyed the huge bed longingly. But it wouldn't do. There were things she had to explain to Jodan Caine—and they had to be said tonight.

Slowly she moved towards the bathroom door and glanced inside. It was as luxurious as she'd expected it would be. The bath was rich blue marble and deep, the fittings were gold. Smoky glass encased the shower, and the wall behind the vanity unit featured bevelled mirror tiles, a complete wall reflecting the entire room.

Her pale, drawn face stared back at her and she drew a shaky breath. She looked ready to drop.

She made herself collect her toiletries and deposit them in the bathroom. Then she opened her suitcase and reached for her nightgown. When she'd packed her case she had almost settled on the oversized T-shirt she usually wore to bed, the one with Garfield the cat emblazoned all over the front, but Jessie's presence had made that impossible. Even the comfort of that well-worn garment was to be denied her, for Jessie had seen the négligé set she'd bought on an impulse especially for her honeymoon. Before that fateful evening when she'd overheard Jodan and Desiree in the garden.

Kasey drew the négligé out of the case now and wondered just what had possessed her to make such a purchase anyway. Painful revelations aside, hers was hardly going to be a proper honeymoon even then. Yet she'd seen it and, without thinking, had bought it.

Ivory satin, floor-length, and the nightgown felt as soft as chamois. When she'd tried it on it had seemed to fall seductively over her bare skin. At the time she rather fancied she'd been trying to convince herself her marriage was to be a real one.

She fingered the silky material. The gown was most definitely of the type chosen by a woman with her lover in mind. With Jodan in mind.

No! She recoiled from her thoughts. Greg—it had been for Greg.

Don't kid yourself, Kasey, scoffed an inner voice. Her old T-shirt seemed synonymous with Greg, but this nightgown was pure seduction, a perfect foil for the smooth, tanned skin of Jodan Caine.

Angrily she strode into the bathroom, locking the door behind her. The warm shower revived her but, when she stepped from the cubicle, she hastily turned her back on the mirrored wall that mockingly reflected her glistening nakedness. Right now, to dwell on the advantages or otherwise of her feminine attributes was the very last thing she needed.

With her nightdress and *peignoir* covering her body, she faced the mirror to brush her red curls into order. Some colour had returned to her cheeks and, of their own accord, and with total disregard for her previous firm intentions, her eyes fell assessingly over her figure.

At least the nightgown wasn't see-through. Her colour heightened. The way the soft material hugged her body it might well have been. Her nipples tingled, thrusting against the fine cloth, drawing attention to the round fullness beneath. Defensively Kasey crossed her arms, before taking a deep calming breath and re-entering the bedroom.

Jodan's case was now open and his discarded shirt hung over a chair. Kasey almost reached out to touch it, then had to stand gathering her shattered composure.

She had to face him, and she had to be unruffled, self-possessed, in total command of herself and the situation.

And a confrontation in the living-room would be far preferable to the intimacy of this bedroom and its huge, so-inviting king-sized bed.

Quickly slipping her bare feet into soft satin mules, she stepped into the hallway.

'White, no sugar.' He held out the mug of steaming coffee and Kasey nodded her thanks, knowing she was incapable of speech just at that moment.

He must have used the bedroom while she had been showering, for he was wearing the same towelling robe he'd worn the morning she'd awoken in his bed. And he was no less attractive now than he had been then. He was devastating, even at a dozen paces.

His feet were bare, as were his legs, and he had good legs, well shaped and firmly muscled, quite sparsely haired for one so dark. As he leant across to pass Kasey her coffee his lapels gaped and her eyes seemed glued to the expanse of broad chest and tanned midriff, the light mat of fine dark hair.

'Come and sit down.' He indicated the soft, inviting-looking lounge chairs and Kasey chose a single-seater opposite him. 'I'd open the drapes but it's pitch-black out there with the rain and clouds, so you'll have to wait until the morning to see the view.' He paused, then continued softly, 'We have the same view from the bedroom.'

The bedroom. We. His words said it all. He really did expect to share her bed. But they were virtual strangers. Kasey shivered and took a gulp of her coffee.

Jodan sighed tiredly and sat back, crossing one bare ankle over the other. 'I'm glad it's all over, aren't you?'

'Yes. No. I mean——' Kasey stuttered, and he watched her with indulgent amusement.

'Relax, Kasey,' he said easily. 'I'm not about to jump at you like a caveman and haul you off to my cave. Not until we've finished our coffee, anyway,' he added drolly.

'Jodan, we should talk. I meant to before today, but there never seemed time and the opportunity didn't arise.' Kasey drew a quick, shallow breath. 'I don't think we should rush into anything.'

His dark eyebrows rose and his eyes narrowed. He took a slow sip of his coffee before speaking. 'What particular thing are we not to rush into?'

'Well... marriage.'

'Isn't it a little late to not want to rush into marriage?' he asked mockingly.

'I didn't mean our marriage, that is, the ceremony, today. I meant we—well, we shouldn't... We scarcely know each other, and we shouldn't... I don't think we should...' Her voice failed her completely as her throat dried.

'Shouldn't?' he repeated matter-of-factly. 'Shouldn't what?'

'You know.' Kasey spread her hands. 'Shouldn't——' she gulped a breath '—sleep together,' she finished quickly.

His cold blue eyes held hers, no hint of humour in them now. 'What are you trying to say, my dear? Separate beds or just no sex?'

Kasey flushed crimson. 'I don't think we should complicate things by rushing into a physical relationship before we get to know each other.'

'I know you, Kasey.'

She gave a quick, agitated shake of her head. 'Look, Jodan, when I said I wanted a husband and you offered to marry me I really didn't expect it would—the actual wedding would take place so soon, and——'

'I wouldn't have agreed to marry you if I hadn't thought it would work,' Jodan said evenly. 'And there's no better way to get to know each other than in bed.'

'For a man, maybe. But it's different for a woman. I don't—well, I don't feel I know you, Jodan, and I can't—I couldn't...' Kasey shook her head again.

'You could have, and you wanted to the night you passed out on me,' he said quietly.

'I was dr—I was depressed that night, I told you so.' Kasey stood up agitatedly. 'I'm sorry, Jodan, I can't sleep with you. You must see it wouldn't be the sensible thing to do, and apart from that, I'm not—I'm afraid I'm not in love with you.'

There, she'd said it, put it into words. She watched him warily.

Slowly he placed his coffee-mug on the table by his chair and just as deliberately rose to his feet. 'What has love got to do with it?' he asked, a steely thread of bitterness binding his words together.

'It's got everything to do with it.'

Jodan gave a short, cynical laugh. 'Surely you don't imagine every couple who indulge in sexual relations are in love with each other? Do you think I've been in love with every woman who's shared my bed?'

A cold finger of pain clutched at Kasey's chest. And I'll bet there've been any number of them, she wanted to throw at him. But she clamped her lips tightly together.

His eyes were locked with hers. 'You think love's a prerequisite for the physical act?'

'As far as I'm concerned——' Kasey swallowed '—perhaps it is.'

'You can't have sex with a man you don't love, is that it?'

Kasey nodded.

His gaze held hers for immeasurable seconds before he turned suddenly from her. 'Why in hell did you want this marriage, Kasey—or perhaps I should say any marriage?' he asked, his back to her, stiff and formidable.

Why? Kasey blinked, trying to clear her mind. What could she say? To show Greg she could find someone too? That she didn't need him? To make him jealous? Jealous enough to change his own plans. Jealous enough to break his engagement to Paula and marry Kasey herself. Just the way she'd always imagined it would be.

But it had got out of hand. And now she'd married Jodan Caine. And just what had it achieved? Oh, Greg had been jealous all right. But not enough to be swayed from his future as boss of Winterwood Station.

'It was—I guess it was a spur-of-the-moment thing,' she began through stiff lips.

'It seemed like a good idea at the time?' Jodan bit out sarcastically.

'Something like that.'

'I don't believe you, Kasey,' he said with ominous softness, facing her again now. 'I'm afraid I don't believe you.'

'Well, it's true.' Her voice sounded thin in her ears and he laughed harshly.

'You're a poor liar, my dear. And I'm not the fool you obviously think I am.'

'What . . . What do you——?'

'I mean I know why you wanted a husband.'

Kasey's startled eyes flew to his. He couldn't know!

'But no matter. That's immaterial.' He shrugged irritatedly. 'The point is that you did marry me, Kasey. Our marriage suited me. And I'm afraid you're going to have to make the best of it.'

Her mouth opened slightly in surprise. 'What exactly do you mean?' she asked him slowly.

He smiled, but there was no amusement in the quirk of his mouth. 'I think you know that, Mrs Caine. You see, I married you in good faith, Kasey. I want a wife. To act as hostess when I need one for business dinners. To manage my home. And to warm my bed.'

'You can't make me...' Kasey swallowed, very aware now of their isolation. 'You wouldn't force me to do something I didn't want to do, against my will.'

'Oh, believe me, you'll want to,' he said softly, his face set aloofly, all arrogant male. 'You're my wife, Kasey. That's how it is and that's how it's staying, so you'll have to get used to the idea.'

'Jodan, this is ridiculous, and I'm too tired to discuss it any further now. I'm going to bed.' With that she walked purposefully past him, up the steps and along the hallway, slippers slapping reassuringly on the tiles.

Yet for all her outward calm her heart was racing, and when she reached the sanctuary of the bedroom her body slumped. She caught at the open door for support while she drew a steadying breath.

She was exhausted now and she moved like a zombie, closing the door, kicking off her mules, slipping out of her *peignoir*. She had just folded back the quilt when the door opened. Kasey started in surprise, her eyes meeting Jodan's cold blue ones across the room. Neither of them spoke for long, leaden seconds.

'I'm going to bed,' Kasey mouthed again, her voice hollow and strained.

'So am I,' Jodan said easily, and stepped into the room. 'With you.'

Kasey straightened, the bedclothes slipping from her nerveless fingers. 'No.' The word breathed from between her stiff lips.

Jodan raised one dark eyebrow. 'I think, yes.'

Somehow Kasey made herself move around the end of the bed. To confront him? Or to be closer to the door and escape? For some crazy, irrelevant reason she noticed that the rain had stopped, that the digital clock radio showed one a.m., that there was a cream telephone by the bed. Perhaps she could reach it, call... Call who?

She stopped a pace or two from him, her bare feet sinking into the deep pile of the carpet, unaware of the picture she made in her ivory nightgown—her slim, gently rounded hips, her firm breasts thrusting forward, her hair falling in a cascade of burnished fiery curls over her smooth creamy shoulders. And her eyes, deep rusty brown, large and luminous in her pale face.

'I don't believe you mean this, Jodan... I can't somehow see you resorting to rape.' How could she speak so calmly when her heartbeats fluttered so apprehensively?

'Rape?' He gave a cold laugh. 'No, I don't force myself on women, Kasey. I don't have to.'

'No?' She managed to add an edge to her voice.

'No,' he restated firmly.

'If this isn't forcing yourself on me, then I don't know what is!'

He held her gaze for long seconds before sighing, looking suddenly bored with the whole conversation. 'Your maidenly virtue is safe for the moment, Kasey. You're tired. I'm tired. We both could use some sleep. And we have shared a bed before to do just that, to sleep.'

Kasey stood undecided, her imagination flashing disturbing pictures before her. Jodan without his robe, his taut, masculine body beside hers on the white satin sheets. Turning to her.

She gave a slight shake of her head and her red curls bounced. It was a tantalising, outrageous thought.

'Go to bed, Kasey,' he said wearily, and disappeared into the bathroom.

Slowly Kasey retraced her steps and slid beneath the sheets, arranging the folds of her nightgown around her. Her whole body was stiff, her muscles refusing to relax. In fact, she was so keyed up she almost cried out when the bathroom door opened and Jodan re-entered the room.

Without a word he flicked off the main lights, leaving only the bedside lamp glowing subduedly.

Hastily Kasey averted her eyes as he untied the belt of his robe, the sound of the discarded material falling on to the nearby chair seeming to echo about the room. She squeezed her eyes closed as the bed moved as Jodan climbed in beside her.

He sighed deeply as he stretched out. He must be tired too, she conceded. On top of the strain of the wedding he had had the long drive up here in far from ideal motoring conditions.

Jodan shifted, settled into the comfortable mattress, his bare leg accidentally brushing Kasey's. She couldn't control her immediate recoil as she moved closer to her edge of the bed.

'Oh, for heaven's sake!' Jodan sat up and turned towards her, the bedside lamp softly illuminating the muscular contours of his broad shoulders, the flatness of his midriff.

A spiral of tingling sensations rose from the pit of her stomach, making her heartbeats quicken disconcertingly. She could barely drag her eyes from the beauty of his taut, male contours, and in that moment she could have begged him to make love to her.

And her thoughts took her completely by surprise. She'd never made love with a man. Yet there had to be a first time. So why not with someone who was undeniably good-looking, masculine, experienced? A man like Jodan Caine.

Kasey drew a short, ragged breath. Dear God! It would be so easy to allow his physical attractiveness, his irrefutable magnetism, to override her own personal moral convictions. Her lips thinned in wry self-derision.

The light blueness of his eyes brightened, burning angry pools in his set face as he gazed down at her. Then his body was blocking out the light as he leant suddenly over her, one hand on either side of her head, biceps bulging beneath his smooth skin as they took his weight.

'Jodan, don't——' Kasey began, fear replacing her traitorous yearnings.

'You know, every provocative line of your beautiful body is crying out for love, Kasey, yet the expression on your face, in your eyes, tells me you're so bloody sure I'm about to ravish you that I don't think I could convince you you're wrong no matter what I said. So perhaps the time for words has passed. And besides, who am I to disappoint a lady?' His lips swooped downwards to claim hers before she had the slightest chance to turn her head away.

'No!' she cried out into his marauding mouth, her hands struggling from beneath the covers to push against the rock wall of his chest. All reason cried out against his assault as she twisted her body beneath him, to no avail. His hands imprisoned hers, held each one just above her head with consummate ease. Panic rose inside her as she realised that physically she was no match for his muscled strength.

Then he lifted his head, his breathing shallow and ragged, his eyes falling from hers to the flutter of her breasts beneath the thin material of her nightgown as she herself fought for breath. For timeless seconds he watched her through narrowed lids.

Overriding her alarm, a stealthy warmth grew inside her, confusing her, momentarily stilling her panic-filled struggles.

His lips descended again, with slow precision, teasing her mouth, his tongue-tip slipping coaxingly between her stiff lips before it slid downwards, nuzzled the hollow of her throat, nibbled across the cream skin of her bare shoulder, expertly pushed aside the material of her nightgown. It sought out the valley between her breasts and lingered tinglingly there. Then slowly, with agonisingly unhurried, feather-soft movements, it began the climb upwards to claim one rosily erect peak. No! No! cried her reason. But her body seemed to have a mind of its own.

His dark hair had fallen forward over his brow and it brushed her skin, teased her senses. She shivered violently, the intensity of her response shocking her into some semblance of time and place.

'No! Jodan, please. This is so wrong!'

'So right,' he murmured against her, shifting his caresses to her other waiting breast. 'So right. So beautiful.'

Somehow her nightgown, so carefully secured about her, had ridden up over her thighs, and she felt the bareness of his skin against hers, the rasp of the fine hair on his leg. His hands that had been holding her arms over her head now released her, slid downwards, found each sensitive, responsive, unawakened part of her. And her body continued to betray her as she fought for control.

Jodan raised his head to look at her again. They were both gasping for breath, and Kasey clamped her softly trembling lips together.

He was contemptible, she told herself—tried valiantly to tell herself.

All the anger had left his face, the cold steeliness gone, to be replaced by a far more potent emotion. The hard line of his mouth had softened noticeably and a dull flush now coloured the line of his cheekbones.

And what of herself? Kasey wondered. Was she too glowing with this undeniable urgency, this need for a fulfilment so unfamiliar and yet so craved? It's purely physical, she reminded herself, while that same indefinable spark continued to glow, to grow, rising to wash away her last vestiges of control.

That perfidious part of her registered the feel of him, the hard contours of his body lying half on and half off her own. The abrasion of his skin seared her sensitised nerve-endings as she endeavoured to pull herself together.

What was wrong with her? Had she gone completely mad? This man was using his superior strength to—— Liar! a voice inside her jeered harshly.

She stirred restlessly, with resistance or response she couldn't have said, and she was just as suddenly, shockingly aware of his arousal.

The corners of Jodan's mouth, those lips that could tantalise and torture, quirked almost self-derisively. 'A man can take only so much provocation, Kasey,' he said softly, still restraining her beneath him. 'Especially on his wedding night,' he added lowly. 'Now we have to decide whether or not we're going to finish what we've started.'

'*I* didn't start anything,' she retorted with some of her old fire.

'Didn't you?'

'No!' She was indignant, and he gave a low, husky laugh.

'You said you were a virgin,' he continued softly. 'Was that the truth or simply the line you tossed me at the time?'

Kasey felt her colour rise and she swallowed, fighting to dislodge the breath that had caught in her throat.

'I could be excused in this day and age for doubting your words,' he began.

'It was the truth,' she got out. 'It *is* the truth.'

Some fleeting emotion flickered across his face. Perhaps he was going to reconsider, Kasey thought. Knowing she was inexperienced——

'Then I'll try not to hurt you,' he said, dashing her moment of reprieve. 'But don't make it any harder, Kasey. Don't fight me.'

His words came out thickly, then he slowly lowered his head to again touch his mouth to the curve of her shoulder, teeth and tongue rekindling the fire that still burned, poised to break control.

'Jodan, we shouldn't— I don't think we should——' Kasey mumbled incoherently as she fought to put her thoughts into words. But the words skittered about inside her mind like crazily bouncing rubber balls, ricocheting away as she tried to grasp them into order.

Her skin felt hot, all aglow, as Jodan's lips slid along her jawline, rose to touch her eyelids, her brow, her nose, until she felt she'd go mad if he didn't kiss her mouth.

When he did, her lips opened of their own volition, allowing him ready access to the sweetness within.

Kasey murmured deep in her throat, a sound she barely recognised as coming from herself, and she blushed at the raw sexuality of its impatient urgency. She made no demur as he removed her nightgown, letting his eyes move with his hands over the long length of her.

'My God! Your skin's like alabaster,' he breathed. 'So perfect.'

His murmured caresses, his tantalising fingertips, inflamed her until she was mindless, completely carried away by her abandoned arousal.

Some tiny fissure of consciousness tried to warn her to be wary, to remind her of the foolishness of her wantonness, but by now she was helpless, unable to call a halt to the sheer exhilaration of his lovemaking.

Only when he moved his body over hers did she stiffen slightly, regaining some small grasp on the significance of her actions.

'Kasey, please.' Jodan's breath teased her earlobe. 'Don't try to stop me now, because I'm afraid I couldn't if I wanted to,' he said thickly.

A moment or a millennium later, Kasey lay on the bed beside him as his breathing slowed. Her body ached, throbbed, and she suspected she would bear the bruises within hours. Was it always so painful? she wanted to ask him, but pride held her tongue. What had gone wrong? At first it had been wonderful, but when the moment had come she had panicked, fought him, and...

'Kasey.' He raised himself on one elbow beside her, gazing down at her. His dark hair fell forward on his damp brow and his eyelashes fell to shield the expression in his eyes.

She turned her head away, ashamed of herself, at the ease with which he had overcome her determined resolutions.

'Kasey,' he repeated harshly. 'Look at me.'

She felt for the sheets, tried to draw them up to cover her nakedness, but he snatched them from her. His hand reached out for her chin, firmly moving her head so that she was forced to meet his narrowed gaze.

'Don't go quiet on me,' he began, and Kasey's lips thinned. He bit off an angry expletive. 'Say something! At least demand an apology,' he retorted hardly.

Kasey relaxed a little and his fingers freed her. Slowly her eyes rose to his and he shook his head.

'You probably deserve one,' he added self-derogatorily, running one tanned hand through his hair.

He pushed himself up into a sitting position and Kasey's eyes followed the play of muscles in his back, noted with no little horror the red scratch-mark across his shoulder-blade. Her hand moved to touch it, soothe it, but she pulled it back.

He sighed and turned back to her, his eyes flickering downwards over her breasts before rising to meet her gaze. 'I'm sorry if I hurt you, Kasey,' he began, and to her mortification Kasey felt a tear swell and overflow on to her cheek.

As her vision blurred she could have sworn a fleeting flash of pain crossed his face.

'Don't cry. Believe me, you can't hate me any more than I loathe myself at this moment.' His eyes held hers steadily. 'Are you all right?'

Kasey nodded. 'I...' Her voice died and she swallowed. 'It wasn't wholly your fault,' she got out, knowing what she said was true. She should have left him, gone to another bedroom, locked the door, right at the beginning.

But part of her had wondered at the taste of forbidden fruit.

'My fault? Of course I'm to blame for what happened. We both know that. I know that. I started it and I thought I could handle it.' He gave a mirthless laugh. 'I was going to tease you a little, overcome your prim reserve, then turn over and go to sleep. Quite a game, wasn't it, Kasey? And I managed it beautifully, didn't I?' he finished softly, bitterly. His eyes fell again to the rise of her beasts and he drew a deep breath. 'You're a very desirable woman, Kasey—you must know that. It's no excuse, I know, for my actions, but you have the most incredibly provocative body.' His hand gently cupped one full breast. 'And, God help me, I want to make love to you again.'

Kasey drew back.

'Not tonight,' he said quickly. 'Even I'm not that insensitive,' he added drily. 'Next time will be different, I promise. We'll take more time, choose our time.' He leant over to kiss her, a soft, comforting movement of his mouth on hers. 'Now, we really should get some sleep. It will be morning before we know it.'

He stretched over to flick off the light, and it seemed he had barely settled beside her when the telephone pealed loudly into the darkness, startling them both. Jodan fumbled for the light, then lifted the receiver.

'Jodan Caine,' he said into the mouthpiece, then frowned. 'Calm down, Desiree.'

Kasey sat up, a stab of pain clutching at her heart at the mention of her sister-in-law's name. She sat stiffly as she listened to Jodan's side of the conversation.

'When?' he asked tersely. 'Have you phoned Dad? You'll have to, Desiree. You should have already done that. Where are the girls? Then take them over to Mum and Dad and get up to the hospital. I'll meet you there as soon as I can.' He put down the receiver, his face pale, a worried frown etching his brow.

'What is it?' Kasey asked. 'What's happened?'

'It's David,' Jodan said flatly. 'He's been taken to hospital. They think he's had a massive heart attack.'

'Oh, no!' Kasey's hand went to his arm, but he didn't seem to notice.

'Desiree's hysterical,' he said just as evenly. 'I'll have to go to her.'

CHAPTER SIX

THEIR return journey to the city seemed twice as long as the drive up to the Blue Mountains less than three hours earlier. At least the rain had stopped, but the roads were still wet and shiny, needing Jodan's complete concentration. He drove swiftly but not dangerously.

Kasey wanted to offer him some form of comfort, some reassurance that his brother would pull through, but she was at a loss to know what to say or do. Apart from his initial statement that David had had a massive heart attack, Jodan had not elaborated about the situation. And at the back of her mind were his words, 'Desiree... I'll have to go to her.'

Numbness had lulled Kasey's body into an outward calmness she was far from feeling inside as she silently sat beside Jodan, her hands clasped together in her lap. What did one say to one's husband of a few hours, a husband who had to go to the side of another woman, the woman he really loved?

Kasey cringed inside. It all sounded so melodramatic. But the facts remained.

At first Jodan had wanted her to stay at Valley View and he had been going to arrange for the caretakers to return, but Kasey had insisted on accompanying him back to town. She had no desire to remain at the house alone, waiting for news of David's condition, wondering about Desiree.

And she could hate herself for even allowing thoughts of her sister-in-law to intrude at such a dreadful time, but it was impossible to forget the reckless unscrupulousness of the conversation she'd overheard between Desiree and Jodan that fateful night a few weeks ago, or Desiree's revelations after their wedding. When it came to Jodan, Kasey suspected that Desiree had no conscience at all.

Their cases had not been unpacked, so it had been relatively easy to leave within a quarter of an hour of Desiree's call. Kasey had slipped into a pair of jeans and an oversized sweatshirt, a far cry from the tailored elegance of the going-away outfit she'd worn on the outward journey.

Jodan also wore jeans, and a loose, light knit jumper. Slanting a sideways look at him, Kasey saw the drawn paleness of his face silhouetted by the flash of a street light. His profile was sharp and tense. How she wished she could reach out to him, console him, and yet seek reassurance for herself.

Of what? she asked herself wryly. Of the chances of his brother's recovery? Of his indifference to his brother's wife? And the other purely selfish reason. That she wasn't the failure as a woman she suspected she had been such a short time ago.

She just couldn't get their lovemaking into perspective. Perhaps she had been expecting too much. Modern women were supposed to know all about it, weren't they? Take it all in their stride. Like men did.

Well, she hadn't. She'd been tense and unresponsive. But she hadn't been repulsed. In fact, she'd liked Jodan's kisses, the musky male taste of him before... Kasey shivered.

'Cold?' Jodan's deep voice made her jump.

'Oh! No, not really.' She swallowed. 'Do you feel all right to drive? I mean, if you're tired I could take over for a while.'

'I'm fine.' He moved slightly, tensing his back. 'We should be at the hospital in about twenty minutes.'

They lapsed into silence again, and for Kasey it wasn't a comfortable quiet. It left so much unsaid between them and it was building a barrier, one that had started the night she had met Desiree.

Activity at the hospital was at a minimum, and Jodan parked the car and strode towards the administration block with Kasey hurrying to keep pace with him. The lift took them to the coronary care unit where Jodan's brother had been admitted.

Kasey saw Desiree immediately. Surprisingly she was still dressed in the flame-red outfit she'd worn to the wedding, and she was pacing the clinical corridor, her high heels beating a sharp tattoo on the highly polished floor. Her fair hair was washed white by the lights and she turned as Jodan and Kasey stepped out of the lift. When she saw Jodan she gave a high little cry and flew into his arms.

Kasey stood back, her breath caught in her chest, her heartbeats thudding in her ears.

'Thank God you're here, Jodan,' Desiree was saying breathlessly. 'It's been awful without you. I hate hospitals— can't stand them!'

Jodan put his arms around Desiree's thin form, murmuring soothingly, words inaudible to Kasey. After a few moments he pulled back a little from her. 'Calm down, Desiree. Just tell me what happened.'

'David wasn't feeling well at the wedding. He's been like it for a while. He thought he just had a virus or something.' Desiree sniffed, her violet eyes bright. 'He didn't even want to dance with me, and after you left he wanted to go home.

'I don't get much time to party, Jodan, not any more. Well, David decided to take the girls home and I stayed on for a while. When I—when I got home I found him on the living-room floor. I thought he was dead, Jodan. I... It was awful! I didn't know what to do.

'I ran next door and woke Fred, and he gave David resuscitation while I called you. He's been in there——' Desiree moved her head in the direction of the closed doors at the end of the corridor '—for so long.'

'What did the doctor say?' Jodan asked her carefully, his arms still around her.

'I... He said... Oh, Jodan, I don't know what he said! I was beside myself.' Desiree clutched at his shoulders, and Jodan's hand moved soothingly on his sister-in-law's arms.

'Did you telephone Mum and Dad?'

'Yes, when I got to the hospital, but they weren't there. They were driving Aunt Grace home, I think.'

Gently, Jodan disengaged himself and moved them towards the waiting-room off to the left.

'The doctors are still with him,' Desiree added as they went into the small alcove.

Kasey's footsteps faltered behind Jodan's.

Desiree's two daughters were in the room. Lisa, the younger one, was asleep on a chair, while Shelley, her older sister, sat up straight beside her, her blue eyes large and wide in her face. Jodan said something under his breath and left Desiree to go to the child.

'Hi, sweetie!'

The little girl was in her pyjamas and she wound her arms around Jodan's neck as he lifted her into his arms.

'Daddy's sick, Uncle Jodan,' she whispered, and a huge tear rolled down her flushed cheek.

'I know, pet, and I'm going in to see the doctor now to ask him how your daddy is.' He gave her a squeeze. 'You wait here with Mummy. I'll be back soon.'

Shelley nodded and he set her down, passing Desiree without a word. The little girl stood stiffly where Jodan had left her as Desiree began to pace the floor again.

'I'd give anything for a cigarette. You haven't got one, have you?' Desiree acknowledged Kasey's presence for the first time.

'No, I'm sorry, I don't smoke,' Kasey said as she crossed to the child, taking her small cold hand and leading her back to the seats, sitting her gently down beside her.

'Doesn't smoke—that figures,' Desiree muttered, her words carrying to Kasey.

Kasey made no comment, more aware of the child's fingers clutching at her own, and Shelley made no demur as Kasey lifted her on to her knee. 'Uncle Jodan won't be long,' she said softly, wishing she could find something reassuring to say to set the little girl's mind at rest.

'Will Daddy be all right, Mummy?' Shelley asked flatly.

'Stop asking me that, Shelley!' Desiree snapped. 'I told you I don't know. Just be quiet.'

The little body in Kasey's arms quivered.

'We'll just have to wait until Uncle Jodan comes back,' Kasey said gently.

And Jodan wasn't away long. When he re-entered the small room his eyes went straight to Kasey in a look that caught her in the chest like a blow. Surely David wasn't——?

Desiree had turned towards him, and Shelley watched him too, her body stiffening.

Jodan moved past Desiree to his niece. 'Daddy's pretty sick, sweetie,' he said gently as he crouched down in front of her. 'But the doctors are looking after him.'

'Are they making him better?' Shelley asked.

'They're doing their best.' Jodan didn't prevaricate.

'Does Daddy's chest still hurt?'

Jodan shook his head. 'No. He's had some medicine and now he's asleep.'

'What did the doctors say?' Desiree demanded shrilly, and Jodan turned a silencing look on her before returning his attention to his niece.

'I think it would be a good idea if you and Lisa went home to Grandma's with Aunt Kasey so you can get some sleep too.'

'What will you do, Uncle Jodan? Will you come with us?' Shelley asked solemnly.

'No, I'll stay here to keep your mother company.'

The child nodded slowly, a play of emotions crossing her face. 'I guess Mummy shouldn't be all by herself. She doesn't like being by herself.'

Jodan gently touched her cheek. 'Good girl. Mummy will take you out into the hall to the water fountain—you must be thirsty by now.'

Shelley nodded and slid from Kasey's lap as Jodan stood up. Desiree opened her mouth to protest, but Jodan's set expression had her moving to do as he'd suggested, leaving Kasey alone with her husband and his younger, still sleeping niece.

'Blast Desiree!' he exclaimed between his teeth. 'Those kids shouldn't be here.' He looked drawn now and very tired. 'Do you mind taking the kids to my parents' house?'

'Of course not.' Kasey shook her head. 'How is your brother?'

Jodan grimaced. 'Not good, but better than the doctors first expected he'd be. We'll just have to wait for the tests and whatever.' He sighed tiredly. 'I'll try to reach my parents again before you leave.'

In no time Jodan was settling the children in the car, Desiree standing back opening the packet of cigarettes she'd bought from the vending machine. Her lighter flared, bathing her face in a brief, distorting blaze.

'Mum and Dad will wait at the house until you arrive, then they'll come on to the hospital,' Jodan told Kasey as he clipped Shelley into her seatbelt.

Kasey started the engine. When will I see you? The words caught in her throat in a painful lump. She couldn't voice them, and her hands gripped the steering-wheel to steady their tremor.

Jodan moved around the car to join Desiree.

'There's no reason for your parents to come up here,' Desiree said petulantly. 'There's nothing they can do.'

'They want to be here,' Jodan said flatly, and leant closer to the car. 'Take it slowly, Kasey, even though there shouldn't be much traffic at this hour. And Kasey——' he paused slightly '—I'm sorry about this.'

'Yes.' Desiree gave a harsh laugh, 'not the usual way to spend your wedding night, is it? I hope my phone call didn't interrupt anything.'

Kasey felt her face go hot. What would the other girl say if she told her she wished she'd interrupted them fifteen minutes earlier? Then they wouldn't have—— Kasey released the brake and backed slowly out of the car park. In the rear-view mirror she watched Jodan take Desiree's arm and walk her back towards the hospital buildings.

The lights blazed at the Caine home and Jodan's parents met Kasey as she drew the car to a halt. John Caine lifted the now sleeping Shelley from the car while Kasey carried Lisa into the house. They settled the children in bed.

'I just can't believe this.' Margaret Caine swallowed a sob. 'I knew David hadn't been feeling well, I could see it in his face, and he seemed so tired.' She broke down, and her husband slid an arm about her shoulders.

'Jodan said David was resting comfortably.' John Caine's eyes sought Kasey's for reassurance.

'Yes. He was asleep and heavily sedated.'

Margaret shook her head. 'Oh, dear! I just hope——' She closed her eyes and shook her head.

'We should get off to the hospital,' John said gently.

'Yes. Once we see him...' Her words faded as her husband led her towards the door. 'Oh, I quite forgot.' She turned back. 'I've put you in Jodan's old room, Kasey. I thought you might like that.' She clutched Kasey's hands. 'And I'm so sorry your honeymoon's been spoiled like this.'

Kasey squeezed the older woman's fingers. 'Don't worry about that—it can't be helped. And we've got plenty of time.'

Margaret Caine was touching a lace-edged handkerchief to her eyes as she climbed into the car.

A spoiled honeymoon? Kasey sighed as she watched the car drive away. Their honeymoon, hers and Jodan's, one that shouldn't even have occurred, was spoiled before David Caine's sudden attack.

Slowly she closed the door. She was exhausted but couldn't go to bed. She checked on the sleeping children, then returned to the luxurious living-room, sitting in a deep leather chair, staring numbly into space. It wasn't until the first rays of sunlight slanted across the thick pile carpet that she seemed to come alive, or at least her anaesthetised thoughts unfroze and started to skate about in her head.

If David Caine died... No. It didn't bear thinking about. She had been far too young to remember her mother's death and her father was always so well, so energetic, she hadn't given losing him a thought. Perhaps that was selfish. Her father wasn't young any more and... Kasey pulled the direction of her thoughts to a stop. Thinking so morbidly wouldn't help at all.

How would she feel if it had been Jodan lying in that hospital bed, attached to tubes and wires, his vital signs being recorded on a bank of sophisticated machinery? But Jodan was young.

David Caine was only thirty-nine, just four years older than Jodan, she reminded herself, and her hands clasped tightly together.

She stood up. She had to do something or she'd go mad. Make some tea, perhaps?

A noise by the door had her swinging around.

'I couldn't sleep any more.' Shelley stood uncertainly, moving from one bare foot to the other. 'Can I sit with you, Aunt Kasey?'

'Of course.' Kasey crossed to the child. 'I was just going to make some tea. Would you like some fruit juice or milk?'

The little girl nodded and followed Kasey to the kitchen. The Caines' housekeeper wouldn't be in for an hour, so they had the immaculate kitchen to themselves.

'Would you like something to eat?' Kasey asked the child. 'An egg or toast?'

'Some toast, please. I'm not very hungry.' Shelley sipped her milk and watched solemnly as Kasey moved about the kitchen. Then they sat silently side by side eating the toast Kasey had made. Eventually the little girl put down her toast, barely touched, and sighed brokenly.

'Is my daddy going to die, Aunt Kasey?'

Kasey swallowed the lump in her throat. 'I'm afraid I don't know, Shelley. He's sick, but he's in the very best place he can be to help him get better. We just have to wait and hope.'

'His chest hurt really badly when we came home from your wedding party and he had to sit down for a while before he could help Lisa and me get into our pyjamas. I wanted to ring Uncle Jodan, but Daddy said no, we shouldn't bother him. Then he felt a little better and said he was going to bed.' Shelley swallowed. 'Mummy found him on the floor when she came home, and she screamed.'

Kasey felt helpless. What should she say to comfort the child, who sat beside her as composed as an adult but whose eyes were filled with fear?

'Uncle Jodan will look after Daddy, won't he?' Shelley asked hopefully.

The telephone on the wall beside Kasey pealed, and they both started with fright. Kasey almost dropped the receiver as she clutched at it.

'Kasey!' Jodan's voice sounded incredibly weary and her knuckles whitened as she waited for him to continue. 'I didn't wake you, did I?'

'No. Shelley and I were just having some breakfast. How's...how's David?'

'Resting comfortably, officially.'

Kasey expelled the breath she was holding and Shelley's hand slid into hers.

'A lot better from where I stand,' Jodan went on. 'I've spoken to him and he's gone back to sleep again. But the doctors are optimistic.'

'That's wonderful.' Kasey squeezed Shelley's hand reassuringly.

'He's been lucky, the doctors told me. This attack was a warning and could have been so much worse. They tell me they won't know for sure until they finish the tests, but he should recover completely. Of course, it'll take time and he'll have to slow down, take a back seat for a while.'

'Will he be in hospital long?'

'Depends on how he goes in the next few days. Anyway, I'll be home soon.' He paused for a fraction of a second. 'I'm taking Desiree to her place to change and rest, then I'll come on and change myself.'

'All right. I'll see you then,' Kasey said stiltedly.

'Is Daddy better?' Shelley asked as Kasey replaced the receiver.

'He's much better, but he still has to stay in hospital for a while.'

A weight seemed to lift from the child's shoulders and she sighed softly. 'Can we go to see him now?'

'Let's wait until Uncle Jodan comes home and we'll ask him.'

But Jodan didn't arrive for a couple of hours. Kasey tried not to allow her thoughts to conjure up images of Jodan with Desiree, but after the second hour had passed her heart grew heavier and heavier in her breast. Where was he? Had David taken a turn for the worse? Had Jodan had an accident?

Shelley and Lisa saw the car from their vantage point at the living-room window and raced to the door, opening it wide before Jodan could mount the steps. He swept them both into his arms, answering their babbled questions, his eyes not meeting Kasey's as she stood quietly in the doorway.

He looked tired and drawn, as he must be, his hair a little ruffled, falling forward on to his forehead, the dusky shadow of a day's growth of beard darkening his jawline.

Kasey stood back as he deposited the two little girls on the top step and led them inside, finally sending them off to ask the housekeeper to brew some coffee. He fell into a soft leather chair, his head falling back, his eyes closed. He sighed deeply.

'You must be exhausted,' Kasey ventured, subsiding on to the arm of the chair opposite him.

He opened his eyes then, regarding her through narrowed, red-rimmed lids. 'I had a doze here and there at the hospital.' He ran his hand along the line of his jaw, the bristles of his beard rasping loudly into the silence of the large room. 'But I'll need a shower and a shave before I begin to feel half-human again.'

'You should get some sleep too.' Kasey felt a hysterical giggle rise inside her. Who would guess they had only been married for less than twenty-four hours? Shouldn't she be in his arms, soothing the tired furrows from his brow? Any conventional wife... But theirs wasn't a conventional marriage and she wasn't an ordinary wife.

'I'll have a snack and then rest for a couple of hours,' Jodan was saying. 'David wants to see the girls, so I said we'd take them up to the hospital later this afternoon. We can collect Desiree on the way.'

Desiree. Kasey swallowed. 'Are your parents going to stay at the hospital?'

Jodan nodded. 'Until we go back.'

'And is David really out of danger?'

'Up to a point.' Jodan grimaced. 'The next few days are crucial. But the doctors are hopeful he'll make a complete recovery—if he takes their advice. Now we just have to convince David that Caine Electricals won't come to a standstill while he recuperates.'

'Will your father be able to manage without him?'

'I'll be helping him out.' Jodan stifled a yawn. 'I rang Terry Joseph, my assistant at Caine Computers, and I've done some reorganising so that I can help Dad out for a few weeks, and I see no problems there.'

That had been an understatement, Kasey decided three weeks later. Jodan rarely arrived home before midnight and had left before Kasey was awake each morning. They had moved into Jodan's apartment, and there were times during the day when Kasey forgot she was married.

She was modelling again with the Cable Agency and life was going on rather much like it had when she'd first moved to the city. It seemed she had simply changed flats and flatmates, for that was all Jodan was. He was using the guest-room so he wouldn't disturb her with his late hours.

Disturb her. Kasey sat on the edge of Jodan's huge empty bed, the very same bed she'd woken in that fateful morning that seemed now so long ago. The morning after she'd asked Jodan Caine to marry her.

Tears rolled down her cheeks. It had all been such a mammoth mistake. She should never have married anyone. And, after their disastrous wedding night, what else could she think? She'd read about women who were frigid, who didn't care for sex, yet somehow she had never imagined she could be one of them.

The growing feeling of failure weighed heavily upon her. It had all seemed so romantic in her adolescent fantasies. Yet her one and only experience with Jodan had been far from romantic. And it had been her fault. She had frozen—like an insipid Victorian virgin. An Ice Maiden.

Kasey dashed a fresh wave of tears from her cheek. It had been such a distasteful experience that even Jodan hadn't wanted to repeat it. And heaven knew, she didn't want that either, she told herself firmly. If they'd been in love...

Angrily she paced the bedroom. She pulled the thin white silk robe she'd slipped on when she'd returned from a modelling assignment irritably about her body.

She was a romantic fool—first with Greg Parker, and now with Jodan Caine. But she didn't love Jodan, and he wasn't in love with her. How could he be when he was still in love with his brother's wife?

The depression of self-pity clutched at her and she sank on to the chair before the mirror, her eyes closing as her reflection mocked her. She looked drawn and pale and completely lack-lustre.

How could she have allowed this to happen? she chastised herself all over again. A marriage that was no marriage at all. A husband she barely knew and rarely saw. And all because Greg had decided to marry someone else.

Greg. Kasey tried to picture his handsome face, his fair good-looks, his boyish charm.

A tap on her bedroom door had her starting with fright, and she barely had time to turn around on the chair before the door slowly opened.

'Kasey?'

Her heartbeats skipped, skittered unsteadily. She tried to stand, but at that moment her legs were suddenly weak, unable to hold her weight.

'Kasey,' Jodan repeated, 'I thought you might still be out. I'm glad I caught you.' He stepped into the room, closing the door behind him and resting his shoulders back against it.

Kasey drew herself together, forced herself to rise, hand still clutching the dressing-table for support. 'What...? You're home early.' So mundane, so wifely, she mocked herself relentlessly.

'Yes. I clean forgot about the Mendelsons' party tonight, until Dad reminded me. We're expected to attend. Joe's an old business associate of Dad's and it's a yearly "do".' He glanced at his wristwatch. 'Can you be ready by eight?'

'I... Yes.' Kasey heard the soft quiver in her voice and straightened, moving away from the dressing-table. She hadn't seen Jodan for days, and now he wanted her to pick up the charade and play the dutiful wife. 'I mean, I'm rather tired and I don't really feel like going to a party tonight.'

'I don't either.' Jodan sighed. 'But I'm afraid I'm obligated to go.'

'Can't you go alone?'

There was a moment's heavy silence as Jodan regarded her through narrowed eyes. 'No, I think not, Kasey. We've only been married three weeks. Don't you think that might look a little strange?' he asked drily.

Kasey shrugged. 'Modern marriages seem very flexible, so I don't see why.' She thought she heard a muffled oath as Jodan straightened.

'I don't happen to agree. I'd prefer to go with my wife.'

'That doesn't seem to have bothered you these past few weeks,' she began, and his dark head rose.

'I couldn't leave David and my father in the lurch. I'm sorry about it, Kasey, but you know I've been working.'

'So you tell me.' The words were out before Kasey could draw them back. Spoken softly, but Jodan had still heard them.

'What's that supposed to mean?' he asked just as quietly, moving slowly around the end of the bed to stop within an arm's reach of her.

Kasey swallowed, forcing herself to hold her ground while all instincts insisted she put some space between them. 'I mean, there doesn't seem much point in pretending our marriage is a normal one,' she skirted the question, and Jodan's lips thinned.

'The private side of our marriage, normal or not, is not going to be on public display,' he said clippedly. 'I insist on that.'

'Who cares, anyway?'

'I care.' His deep voice rolled over her, setting her heartbeats dancing wildly.

What was happening to her? When he was near her she began losing control, losing herself... 'When you feel like it,' she bit out, as angry with herself now as she was with him. 'When you have time.'

'Kasey, I'm too tired to argue with you, but if you want to start something I'm quite prepared to finish it.'

CHAPTER SEVEN

JODAN'S eyes fell downwards, touched the mutinous curve of Kasey's mouth, slid lower, along the deep V of exposed creamy flesh where the lapels of her robe had parted slightly.

Valiantly Kasey fought the almost overwhelming urge to clutch the folds protectively about her. Surely he wasn't suggesting that she wanted him to——? But before she could collect herself to reply he shook his head, running a weary hand though his hair.

'Kasey.' His deep voice transformed her name into a caress, and she felt all her anger begin to drain out of her. And into the empty void one emotion replaced another. A tiny spiral of sensation rose from the pit of her stomach so suddenly that she wanted to move towards him rather than flee from him.

'I'd like you to come with me.'

Kasey's eyes met his, held, and she began to panic inside. She was drowning, caught in a whirlpool deep in their cool blue depths. Go with him? Just then she would have gone to the ends of the earth with him. And for him.

'Humour me, hmm?'

'All right,' she heard herself say, and he gave a brief crooked smile, his eyes still on her.

'Good. We needn't stay late.' He glanced at his gold wristwatch again. 'It doesn't give us much time to get ready, so I guess I'd better have a quick shower.' He began to remove his tie as he turned towards the door.

*   *   *

Kasey spent some time over her make-up. She had already showered and now only needed to slip into her dress. She had decided on her favourite, a simply cut outfit in a vibrant shade of peacock-blue. And all this trouble she was taking, she told herself firmly as she applied a touch of mascara to her long lashes, was for herself. Not to impress anyone. She felt good if she knew she looked good.

Would Jodan think she looked——? Kasey pulled her thoughts into line before they could continue on that track. Wasn't it enough that she'd allowed him to talk her into going to the Mendelsons' party?

When she finally left the bedroom she knew her appearance was flawless—modelling had taught her that. Jodan was waiting for her in the living-room, straightening the cuff of his shirt as she approached.

If her appearance was faultless, then they were perfectly matched. It took her some considerable will-power to school her features as she gazed at him, pausing, her step faltering as her eyes drank him in. He wore a charcoal-grey soft leather bomber jacket which sat well on the breadth of his shoulders, and his white shirt was a complete foil for the strong tanned neck and his dark hair, still damp from his shower. Tailored trousers, a shade darker than his jacket, moulded his thighs, accentuating the long, powerful length of his legs.

Yes, he was incredibly attractive, and Kasey couldn't deny he appealed to her senses. Aesthetically, she insisted. Physically, Jodan would attract any woman, be she sixteen or sixty.

He turned slightly towards her then and she continued into the room. His eyes flickered, steadied, roved over her. 'You look quite——' he paused '—stunning.'

Kasey's mouth had suddenly dried and she clutched her small evening bag as her body tensed. She recognised the emotion that had burned in his eyes for that split second before his lashes fell to disguise it. He found her attractive, and she wasn't so naïve as to not recognise his desire. At that moment she rather suspected her own hunger matched his. A searing heat raced over her, and her senses, every nerve in her body, signalled red alert.

'You don't look so bad yourself.' Had she actually said the words in that only faintly breathless voice, or simply thought them?

Jodan chuckled, a deep, husky sound that played over her already highly tuned nerve-endings. He gave a slight bow. 'Thank you. Stunning and not so bad. Quite a combination.' He held out his arm. 'Shall we go?'

Kasey slipped her hand into the crook of his arm. But touching him only intensified her body's rampant responses, and when they reached the door she drew away from him, continuing on to the lift keeping some space between them.

He drove carefully through the rush of evening traffic, and the silence stretched, magnified. It had begun in the lift that had taken them from the penthouse floor down to the private car park beneath the building, and grew as they sat side by side in the car, careful now not to touch.

Kasey didn't dare glance at him. Her body was as tight as a coiled spring. Could he feel the tension, the awareness that seemed to thunder in her ears? Had she stood beneath Niagara Falls she couldn't have been more deafened by it. If she didn't say something soon she was sure she might scream. She tried to speak, but only managed a choked cough.

Jodan sighed, and somehow a little of the strain dissipated. 'Traffic jams aside, we should be there in a few minutes,' he said easily, and Kasey wondered if she alone had imagined the extent of strain that had filled the car.

The closeness still gripped her, and even the city buildings seemed to crowd her. At Akoonah Downs the black sky and the bright stars would be giving the impression of a universe that went on forever.

Forever. The word made Kasey suddenly sad and she wished herself back in the country, the outback, in the security of her old life. Without Jodan? The question confused her, caused her chest to tighten. Back with Greg? No, not with Greg.

She gave herself a mental shake. Her sudden turmoil stemmed simply from Jodan's nearness. He was far too attractive, too larger than life, or she had allowed him to take on that ridiculous dimension. Poor Greg—he didn't stand a chance. Greg. His wedding. She'd forgotten the invitation, and telling Jodan about it had slipped her mind.

'I've—that is, *we've* been invited to a wedding on Saturday week.' Kasey's words were almost steady. 'The invitation arrived the week before we—before we were married, and I think I forgot to mention it, didn't I?'

'You did.' There was a smile in his voice. 'But that's understandable.'

'Will you be able to go?'

'Do you want to go?'

'Of course. But it's out at the station— I mean, at the local church near Akoonah Downs, so we'd have to go out there. Can you get away?' Kasey found herself holding her breath, waiting for his reply.

'I don't see why not. And whose wedding will we be attending?' He sounded amused.

Would he remain so if she told him the truth? The wedding of the man I loved, the man I always expected to marry. The man who rejected me the night I asked you to marry me. Kasey swallowed and turned her head slightly, away from her husband, not seeing the passing cityscape.

'One of my father's station-hands,' she said flatly, then realised she could have sounded condescending. 'But he's more like one of the family really. He's a great friend of my brother's.'

'Have I met him?' Jodan asked easily.

'Yes, I think so. He was at our wedding.' Kasey strove to keep her voice even. 'Greg Parker.'

'Ah!'

Was there a hidden meaning in that soft exclamation? Did Jodan know? Of course he didn't. She was being fanciful.

'Parker,' Jodan continued. 'Tall, fair hair. His fiancée's that little dark-haired girl who hangs on his every word.'

'Yes—Greg and Paula.' Kasey swallowed again. 'Paula's father owns the station next to ours.'

'I see.'

But what he saw Kasey didn't have the opportunity, if the inclination, to ask him as he swung the car to a halt in front of their hosts' imposing home.

Half an hour later, after the greetings, introductions, teasing jibes at their newly married state and a lot of small talk, Kasey and Jodan were separated. Not that Kasey minded. Tonight Jodan was having far too overwhelming an effect on her. She felt so very vulnerable to the potent magnetism he exuded. Apart, she might have some chance of gathering her defences together, getting her perfidious feelings into a reasonable perspective.

She circulated for a while, then accepted an orange juice from a passing waiter. As she turned she came face to face with her brother-in-law. 'David, I didn't know you'd be here.' She smiled at him.

'Hi, Kasey! My first outing. Desiree's here somewhere too, although I haven't seen her for a while in the crush.'

And Kasey hadn't seen Jodan. Were Jodan and Desiree together? She firmly pushed the thought to the back of her mind and forced herself to concentrate on David. He was thinner, but looked remarkably well considering his ordeal.

'How are you feeling?' She asked him the question she supposed he'd been answering all evening.

'Fine. Better than I've felt in months. I'm going to spend a couple of hours in the office starting next week.'

'Are you sure you're not rushing it?' Kasey frowned and David laughed, the tilt of his jawline reminding her fleetingly of Jodan.

'You sound like my mother! No, I won't overdo it. I'll be far more stressed if I'm confined to the house now, believe me. Jodan's been great helping Dad out, but he has his own business to attend to and he can't prop us up forever.' He sobered. 'I'm sorry all this postponed your honeymoon, Kasey, but in a few weeks I should be able to take over from Jodan completely. Then you two can get away for a while.'

'Don't worry about that, David. Just concentrate on getting better,' Kasey reassured him, and he nodded.

'Jodan said he was planning a holiday quite soon.' David winked at her. 'But he assured Desiree and me that, even though he's been helping us out at Caine

Electricals, you've made the most of what time you've had together.'

A dull flush washed Kasey's cheeks, much to David's delight, and he squeezed her arm—then was just as suddenly serious.

'He cares for you very much. I didn't believe it would ever happen. I mean, Jodan's never been short of female admirers, but I know he's put all his time into building up his computer business these past eight or ten years. You don't have much time or energy left over for swanning around when you work as hard as he has, I can vouch for that.' A deep frown shadowed his face, but he consciously shed whatever devils had claimed him and grinned again. 'Not that I'm saying he's been living like a monk, but from the time he met you, Kasey— well, you knocked him out.'

'Now, David, don't——'

'Uh-uh!' David shook his finger in front of her. 'Believe it, Kasey. I know my young brother, and it's true.'

Before she had time to collect herself to reply, a couple came up to enquire after David's health and Kasey quietly drifted away, her brother-in-law's revelations spinning inside her head. Jodan must have played his part well with his family. Yet she couldn't push David's words aside.

Somehow it was impossible to imagine the dynamic Jodan Caine not surrounded by a bevy of beautiful women, but to say he was smitten by her—Kasey just couldn't convince herself of that. She tried to cast her mind back to the modelling assignment where she'd actually first seen him. Of course, she'd been so miserable then that she hadn't taken in all that much that had gone on around her. Men had asked her out constantly, but she had had no difficulty declining—thus the Ice Maiden label.

That first evening, she recalled noticing that Jodan had spent some time talking to Betty Cable. In fact, it had been her employer who had introduced them. She remembered recognising his obvious attraction, but she'd excused herself quite quickly after refusing his offer of dinner. On the couple of occasions she had noticed him after that he hadn't seemed to be with any particular female. And that night, that fateful night at the tavern, he'd been alone. Why wouldn't he, when there was Desiree? she reminded herself, and moved through an arched doorway into another room full of people.

She couldn't see anyone she recognised, but the sound of Jodan's name being mentioned stopped her in her tracks. She didn't think she'd seen the couple before. They had their backs to Kasey, unaware of her presence as they stood talking and laughingly refilling their glasses. Kasey didn't mean to eavesdrop, but she couldn't move away.

'I see Jodan Caine and his new wife are here.' The woman's remark had caught and held Kasey's attention.

'Yes. And I notice his beautiful sister-in-law and her long-suffering husband are here as well.' The man chuckled nastily. 'Can't understand how David Caine doesn't even notice his wife's predilection for his brother.'

'Jodan and Desiree were going together before she married David, weren't they?'

'And after, I'd swear.'

'I wonder if Jodan's bride is aware of it. Seems a bit incestuous, doesn't it?'

The man laughed again. 'Maybe it's all off now between Jodan and Desiree. It shouldn't bother her, though—I hear Desiree spreads herself around. Jodan

Caine's not the only fish swimming in that particular pond. Anyway, Jodan would have to be mad. What guy would need to fool around when he has that gorgeous redhead at home?'

'There've been rumours she's a cold fish,' the woman reminded him. 'And I must say I thought there was something funny about that marriage. No one saw them as an item beforehand, and it was all so sudden it had the trappings of a first-rate shotgun affair.'

'Don't think so, ducky. For one, I can't see a guy as clued up as Jodan Caine falling for the oldest trick in the book. And for another, that dress fits the new Mrs Caine's beautiful body like a glove. What I would give for the chance to peel it off!'

'You're a dirty old man, Frank, and I'm madly jealous. Look, there are the Risdales over there, let's go and get all their news.'

The couple moved off, leaving Kasey standing numbly, a fine film of perspiration dampening her brow. She felt decidedly faint, and slowly made her way to the powder-room. So everyone knew about Jodan and Desiree. So much for Desiree's profession of discretion! And the general consensus was that Kasey was pregnant. A naïve little country bumpkin, who didn't have the sense to take precautions. Or perhaps a newcomer to their social scene who had espied the most eligible bachelor and done what she had to do to capture him.

Kasey groaned softly. What despicable people! How she wished she hadn't overheard that particular conversation. She wished—— She bit off an angry expletive and crossed to the ornate basin to splash her face and renew her light make-up. People like that weren't worth worrying about. Yet it took her some time to gather her courage to rejoin the party.

'Kasey, I've been looking for you everywhere.' Jodan materialised beside her, his arm sliding around her waist.

'And now you've found me,' she remarked flatly, and he gave her a quick, sharp glance.

'The band's playing in the ballroom. Would you care to dance?' His lashes lowered warily, or perhaps Kasey was imagining it, reading guilt where none existed. And making excuses for him, she reflected with self-derision.

'Dance?' Her eyebrow rose. 'Why not? I suppose it's expected of us, is it?'

'No, it's not expected. I just thought you might enjoy a break from making conversation,' he replied reasonably, and Kasey let him lead her towards the music.

Half an hour later some of the tension had eased and she had even begun to enjoy moving in step with her handsome husband. She knew they made a striking couple and was aware of the eyes turned on them.

Then the music slowed, softened, lulled, and Jodan moved closer, sliding both arms around her, his breath fanning the sensitive skin by her ear. And the rising response that surged through her spelled danger.

'Jodan, I'm a little tired,' she began.

'Relax, Kasey,' he murmured throatily, and slid his hand down the length of bare skin displayed by the plunging neckline of the back of her dress. His fingers gently probed the hollow of her spine, settled over the creamy smoothness of her back.

She shivered, and knew by the softly expelled breath that he had felt her involuntary movement.

'What's that perfume?' he asked thickly. 'It could drive a man insane.' His lips caught her earlobe, teeth lightly nibbling, before his tongue-tip sought each vulnerably susceptible nerve-ending.

Kasey's knees went weak and she leant against him, her arms sliding upwards around his neck. Through the thin silky material of her dress she felt every movement, each small muscular nuance as they swayed to the slow, sensuous beat.

'Mmm,' Jodan murmured against her. 'You taste divine too, Mrs Caine.'

His hands, one on her buttocks, the other still moving in slow, inciting caresses across her back, combined with his enchanting nearness, the teasing torture of his lips against her earlobe, the heady sensation of his breath in her hair, all wove a silken, sessile web about her. And she melted into him.

Of their own accord her fingers played in the thick darkness of his hair at the nape of his neck, one fingertip, feather-soft, tracing the outline of his ear. His jacket was open and her breasts tightened, grew full, her nipples hardening, thrusting against the thin material of her dress, the thick solid wall of his chest. The whole hard length of him was moulded to her.

And his obvious arousal sent her senses soaring.

Reason, rationality, escaped her. She gave herself up to the wondrous exhilaration of it. As they swayed together, her inhibitions fled as though they'd never existed, and she wanted this moment to go on forever.

Jodan gave a soft, deep-throated moan and his lips slid along her jaw to her mouth, kissing her lightly on one corner and then the other, light, evocative kisses that tortured, tormented, made Kasey want to cry out, beg him to crush her lips beneath his, taste the sweetness within.

The french windows were open and he swept her outside, into the semi-darkness. Leaning back against a white pillar, he pulled her impossibly closer to him and kissed her as she'd never been kissed before, as she'd never in her wildest fantasies imagined she'd be kissed. When he surrendered her lips, they were both gasping for breath.

'I really think, Mrs Caine,' Jodan got out brokenly, 'that we should make haste for home, don't you?'

Kasey nodded, her rusty brown eyes aglow.

'Otherwise we may make something of a spectacle of ourselves. And quite frankly, just at this moment I won't be held responsible for anything that might happen.'

Kasey stifled a giggle as she still rode the crest of the electrifying wave he'd set her upon.

'Just give me a minute or two, to collect myself,' he said with a wry smile. Taking a deep breath, he clasped her hand tightly in his. 'Ready?'

They merged with the partygoers, skirting the throng of dancers, weaved their way through the crush of noisy conversationalists, and had just made their farewells to their hosts when a petulant voice calling Jodan's name checked their departure.

'Jodan! Surely you're not leaving?' Desiree pouted up at her brother-in-law.

'It's late, Desiree. Both Kasey and I have had a long day,' Jodan told her flatly.

'But you said you'd take me home, and I don't want to leave just yet.'

'Then take a taxi,' Jodan suggested shortly. 'Where's David? He shouldn't be out this late.'

Desiree made a dismissing gesture with one small hand. 'Oh, he went home hours ago. I told him I'd come home with you.'

'Well, I'm leaving now.'

Desiree hesitated, and gave a flounce of one bare shoulder. 'Oh, all right—I suppose I'll have to go too.

You can take me home after you've dropped Kasey off. She looks absolutely exhausted.'

Jodan turned a sharp glance on Kasey, a slight frown hovering on his brow. 'Let's go, then,' he said, and they all moved down the broad marble steps.

They were soon in the car and heading homewards. And Kasey had to admire Desiree's effrontery. The other girl had manoeuvred Kasey into the back seat of the BMW while she settled into the seat beside Jodan. Kasey suppressed a threatened giggle. A campaigning general couldn't have carried out a more successful strategy!

Desiree chatted at length about various people at the party, totally ignoring Kasey, while Jodan answered in monosyllables.

Kasey's gaze was drawn to the back of her husband's head and she fought the urge to lean forward, let her fingers linger again in his hair, nuzzle her lips against the smooth, strong neck.

Desiree's hand moved then, reached out to settle intimately on Jodan's arm, rested there, and the sight of those small white fingers gently caressing the dark sleeve of his jacket turned Kasey cold.

Desiree and Jodan—how quickly she'd forgotten! She'd allowed the purely physical attraction she felt for an extremely magnetic man to cloud her thinking. Her heart had overridden her head. No—her body had betrayed her. What she felt for Jodan was pure, unadulterated lust. And she felt as though something was slowly dying inside her.

When Jodan pulled the car into the kerb outside their apartment building, she went numb with disappointment. She slid from the seat without meeting his gaze.

Leaving the engine of the BMW running, he saw her inside the door. 'You do look all in.'

He raised a hand to brush a wave of hair from the side of her face, and Kasey couldn't prevent herself from flinching back from him. His jaw tensed, his eyes meeting hers for one hard, steely second.

'I'll be half an hour,' he said flatly. And he turned on his heel and was gone.

CHAPTER EIGHT

KASEY slowed her horse as she topped the rise, reining to a stop, to sit overlooking the sprawling buildings of Akoonah Downs. She'd been home for a week. A week without Jodan.

When he had returned from delivering Desiree home, nearer an hour later rather than his stated thirty minutes, Kasey had ensured that she had been curled up in bed. She'd heard him approach her door, pause, tap softly, call her name.

How she'd wanted to fly to the door, fling it open, throw herself into his arms, pick up where they'd left off at the party. But she'd refused to allow herself to do that.

The knob had turned, but the door had remained closed on its lock, which she'd resolutely secured.

Part of her had screamed for him to break the door down. But she had been disappointed. The knob had clicked back and his footsteps had receded. So she'd lain in her lonely bed, her body aching for fulfilment, still sleepless as the sky had lightened.

The next day had been a nerve-racking strain. Jodan had kept to his study, working late into the night. And on Monday morning, when Kasey had woken from a fitful sleep, he had gone. There was some problem in the Adelaide branch and he had to fly down there, his note had told her. He could be away for a week. He would phone before he returned.

And she'd spent that day feeling even more wretched than she had the evening before. She'd even called off a modelling assignment because she just couldn't have faced a camera trying to look happy when she had been feeling so very much the opposite.

When Jessie had rung that night to tell her that her father had had a slight accident, it had been all she'd needed to send her bolting for home. Jessie had assured her that Mike Beazleigh had been fine, now that his broken leg had been set, but she had insisted on coming home. On running away.

The bridle jingled as she shifted the reins in her hands, and she took her hat from her head to fan her warm face. The sun was higher in the morning sky now, and Jessie would be grumbling about her galloping off without having breakfast.

Her eyes roved her childhood home. The main house was typical of its kind, a large, comfortable, single-storey building with a high-pitched roof and surrounded by wide verandas in deference to the heat of summer, when the temperatures reached well over a hundred degrees Fahrenheit.

Kasey's great-grandfather had built the house, and with foresight had planted lots of trees around the building, gums now straight and tall, surviving despite the dryness of the area.

Her father was seated on the veranda in his favourite squatter's chair, plastered leg propped up on one of its characteristic extended arms. Jessie had set the small table beside him for their morning cuppa.

Mike Beazleigh waved as Kasey passed on her way to the stable, where she unsaddled and rubbed down her old horse before striding back to join her father on the veranda.

'You're a bit late this morning,' her father said as she walked up the half-dozen weathered wooden steps that had worn smooth over the years. 'You missed your phone call.'

'Phone call? Who was it?' Kasey stopped, her hand unconsciously going out to clasp the veranda post for support. A sinking sensation clutched at her and she somehow knew exactly what her father was going to say.

'Your husband.'

Kasey swallowed. 'Oh,' she managed through suddenly dry lips.

'He's arriving tomorrow,' Mike told her, his casually spoken words hitting her like a thunderbolt.

Jodan was coming here to Akoonah Downs? It was the very last thing she'd expected him to do. Why would he do that?

A fine film of perspiration that had nothing to do with the warming air around her dampened her forehead, and when Jessie joined them, carrying a large plate of homemade fruit cake, Kasey hurriedly excused herself, the thought of food turning her stomach.

Why was he following her?

She spent the first sleepless night she'd had since returning to Akoonah Downs, and didn't even go for her usual early morning ride on Minty.

Now she sat in front of the mirror in her bedroom, and absently combed the tangled mass of red curls into some order.

'Go and get yourself prettied up, girl,' Jessie had said. 'He'll be here any time now, if the plane's on schedule.'

Prettied up. If Jessie only knew! Out here there was no need for her to be on show as the model Katherine Beazleigh, or as the envied Mrs Jodan Caine. There were no gossip columnists, no scandalmongers on Akoonah Downs. It was all a phoney fiasco. To Jodan she was just the symbol of a wife. And a fairly flimsy smoke-screen for the affair he was having with his brother's wife.

It was the reason he'd married her. Oh, she didn't doubt the fact that physically he desired her—an added bonus for him, surely. Even if their first—Kasey searched derisively for the correct description of their wedding night—their first physical encounter had been such a failure. She moaned softly as a mixture of sensations returned to taunt her—agitation, fear, pain, humiliation. An overall sense of failure.

Then that night at the party played over in her mind. She was in Jodan's arms, moulded to the long length of him, burning for him to make love to her, right there on the dance floor if he'd chosen to do so.

Kasey dropped her brush on to her dressing-table and sprang to her feet. Now Jodan was coming here to Akoonah Downs. Why? She needed more time on her own, away from their magnificent penthouse, their crazy marriage. Away from him. She wanted to evaluate her life with no distractions. How could she do that in his disturbing presence? That was why she'd had to get away. And she needed to escape now.

Grabbing her hat, she headed through the kitchen to the back door. She wasn't ready to face him.

'Where on earth are you going, Kasey?' Jessie demanded in surprise.

'For a ride. Just up to the top of the rise.'

'But Jodan will be here any minute,' Jessie began, moving around the large, scrubbed wooden table, wiping her hands on her floral apron.

'I know. I won't be long, I promise. I'll see the plane land from up there.'

Kasey ran down to the stable and saddled up Minty, cantering up the gentle incline towards the hill behind the homestead. She stopped in the patchy shade of a clump of trees and, dismounting, she screwed up her eyes, searching the endless cobalt-blue sky for the speck that would materialise into a small plane.

She heard it before she saw it, and she watched as the pilot made his approach, dropped off height through the heat haze and taxied to a halt at the end of the runway, partly shrouded in his cloud of dust.

Billy Saturday slid the station's battered four-wheel-drive to a halt and waited while the passenger stepped down from the plane.

Her breath caught in her chest as she watched Jodan stride across to the dusty jeep and throw a small bag into the back before climbing up beside the Aboriginal stockman. Billy dropped him off at the homestead and he disappeared beneath the overhanging veranda roof. Now her father and Jessie would be welcoming him.

Her instinct was to flee, just gallop away over the plains, but she was transfixed, glued to the spot, knowing he had seen her silhouetted here just as surely as she had seen him.

And even when he strode down to the stables and reappeared leading one of the horses, swinging agilely up into the saddle, starting up the hill towards her, she remained motionless, incapable of making her escape.

He reined the horse when he reached her and slipped from the saddle to walk a little stiffly towards her. 'Hello, Kasey.' His deep voice vibrated through her. 'Jessie said I'd find you here.'

'I was... I came out riding.' Her own voice wasn't nearly as composed, as self-possessed as his. 'You shouldn't have ridden up here. I was about to come down.' The words tumbled out, unsteady and uneven.

'I thought we needed to talk.' He'd stopped a few feet away from her. 'In private.'

'I'm sorry I wasn't able to reach you at your hotel in Adelaide——' Kasey began.

He moved his hand negatingly, a flicker of irritation crossing his face. 'That's not why I'm here.' His eyes were narrow slits against the glare of the outback sun. 'Do you want a divorce?' he asked her flatly.

'A divorce?' she repeated softly, her own eyes lifting to stare in shocked surprise at his ruggedly chiselled profile. Never in a million years would she have expected this.

'A divorce.' He turned his head to face her. 'The dissolution of the marriage contract. Isn't that what your timely bolt for home and family is all about?'

Every hard, taut line of his body spoke anger, perhaps more frightening in that it was an anger held under tight, steely control. This was a Jodan Caine she had never seen.

'I came home because my father needed me.' She raised her chin defensively, knowing inside herself that her father's accident was only part of the reason she had returned to Akoonah Downs. But divorce?

'OK.' He inclined his dark head. 'Point taken. But I have a gut feeling your father's misfortune was the excuse you'd been waiting for, justification if you like, for putting as much space as possible between us. So——' he rested his hands on his hips '—what about an answer to my question? Do you want a divorce?'

'I don't... I hadn't thought...' She tripped over her words, trying to sort out her numbed feelings. Had she really allowed herself to think as far along the track as the termination of their marriage? A divorce after a month? Possibly the shortest marriage in memory.

'Surely it must have crossed your mind.' An edge of sarcasm touched his tone.

Getting away from him had, she admitted to herself. But not in quite the cold terms of divorce. More as a panic-stricken need to escape.

Her lips thinned unconsciously. The fact that they had married at all was no one's fault but her own. On many occasions before the day she'd wanted to call the whole thing, the whole fiasco, off. But she hadn't. Even when she'd overheard his conversation with Desiree... She bit her lip, pushing that particular scene from her mind.

And then on their wedding night... She could barely bring herself to think about it. How she'd desperately wished she'd been any place on earth than in his bed. And afterwards...

He moved, startling her out of her tortured retrospections. Taking a couple of strides away from her, he rested one hand on the gnarled low limb of the tree that offered them some small measure of dappled shade.

'We haven't exactly made a roaring success of this match of ours, have we?' he asked quite casually, as though he were discussing the weather, and he didn't so much as cast a sideways glance at her.

'I suppose not,' she conceded quietly. 'But——' Why was she hesitating? Shouldn't she be jumping for joy at his suggestion that they go their separate ways? It would be the civilised thing to do under the circumstances. If they were free... She put an immediate stop on that train of thought. Being free wouldn't help either of their situations. What a hopeless mess it all was!

'But?' he prompted.

'My father will be upset,' she murmured abstractedly.

He turned back to face her, but his dark lashes shielded the expression in his eyes. His lips twisted wryly. 'Will he?' His tone implied disbelief, and she coloured faintly.

'Of course.'

'Perhaps he will. He's a caring father. But he was also upset when we married.'

'Only because we'd not known each other for very long. He thought we were rushing the wedding, that we should have waited.'

'And it seems he was right.'

Kasey made no comment, her fingers nervously playing with the sliding bead on the leather thong holding her wide-brimmed hat in place.

Yes, they should have waited. Waited! Kasey had to suppress a slightly hysterical gurgle of mirth that rose within her, threatening to burst from her. Yet at this moment she couldn't have felt less like laughing. The whole thing should never have gone past her ridiculous statement, made when she had been distraught and slightly under the weather, that she'd needed a husband.

'I suppose I can understand how he felt.' Jodan's voice startled her out of her painful reflections again, and when he noticed her enquiring surprise he explained, 'Your father—I can understand how he felt. You are his only daughter. I could make a pretty fair sort of guess that he wanted you to marry a man of the land, someone like himself. At least, he gave me that impression.' He paused, continuing to watch her, and she shifted uneasily. 'I'm city born and bred. Not your father's cup of tea at all.'

'I wouldn't say that exactly.'

'No? You're being kind, my dear.' His face held the expression of cold arrogance she'd only previously heard in his voice when he spoke to Desiree.

'My father likes and admires you, as I'm sure you know. Any reluctance on his part was, as I told you, because we were—well, because the wedding was so rushed.'

He gave a harsh laugh. 'We didn't exactly have the longest of engagements, did we? When he flew in the day before the wedding, your brother confronted me with the sixty-four-thousand-dollar question, did you know that?'

'What question?' Her brow furrowed.

'Did you take advantage of my sister and put her in the family way?'

She felt the burning heat of a fully fledged blush rise over her cheeks, and she bit her lip to still its tremble.

'Quite a joke, wasn't it, under the circumstances, considering we'd barely kissed?' She watched his eyes settle momentarily on her mouth. 'Although, as I said at the time, I did wonder if pregnancy was the reason for your fervent proposal.'

'It wasn't. And I'm sorry if you were—if my father and Peter——' she swallowed '—if you were embarrassed by it all.'

'I was flattered, Ice Maiden,' he murmured softly, and her eyes swung to his face, a funny little pain squeezing in the region of her heart. 'And I'm not that easily embarrassed.'

'I... We... I won't know how to... what to tell my father——' Kasey began.

'He'll take it, Kasey. And he'll see it as a situation where he's been proved right. He asked me to give our engagement more time. Now he can say "I told you so".'

'My father's not like that at all!' she burst out, and Jodan shrugged.

'He has every right to. We hadn't known each other for long.' He paused. 'Not as long as you'd known Parker, for instance.'

Kasey's eyes rose to meet his in unfeigned surprise, and when she realised what he'd said she felt herself flush guiltily. Her gaze fell from his and she turned slightly, the sound of her riding-boot shifting on the dry, gravelly ground echoing loudly in the silence between them.

'I gather you all grew up together?'

She shrugged. 'Dad treated Greg like another son.'

'But not quite a son.'

She looked back at him then, a slight frown on her brow.

'Your father never adopted him.'

'No, of course not. How could he? Greg has parents in Western Australia, but he——' she shrugged again '—they don't get on. He left home when he was fifteen and a year later he turned up here on Akoonah Downs looking for work. Dad hired him and gave him a chance. No one else ever had.'

'How old were you then?'

'Not very old.' But she'd fallen in love with Greg, with his fair, boyish good looks, from the moment she'd first seen him standing on the veranda in his faded, almost threadbare jeans, his battered, dusty hat clutched in his hand. 'I was about eight,' she added introspectively.

Jodan was watching her with those piercing, so-cold blue eyes, and she felt a flush colour her face again. She could almost believe he had read her mind, knew every detail she had tucked away in its secret cache of precious memories.

'So your father took him in and taught him all he knew.'

'I suppose so. Greg learned right alongside my brother. They were the best of friends, Greg and Peter. Well, the three of us were.'

'Just good friends.'

'Yes, we were.'

He smiled, a chilling upward flicker of the hard line of his lips as his eyes held hers. 'I don't think so, my dear. Not you and Greg Parker.'

'What are... What do you mean?'

'I saw the way Parker looked at you at our wedding. If I hadn't known he was engaged to someone else, I'd have said he was pretty hopelessly in love with you.'

'Well, you were mistaken.' Her heartbeats rose in her chest, threatening to choke her.

'Was I?'

'Yes, you were.'

The cold smile touched his mouth again. 'What happened between you and Parker? Did you have a lovers' tiff? And then perhaps you ran off to the city expecting him to follow after you and beg you to come home.'

This was a nightmare. Was this conversation really happening?

'No, of course not. Why should I do that?'

'To bring him to heel. To have him beg you to come home.'

'That's ridiculous! You don't know a thing about me, about my life.'

'No, I don't, do I? But I do know there was more than friendship in Parker's eyes when he looked at you as you walked down the aisle. So...' He rubbed his jaw with his hand, a long, artistic hand, with clean, clipped nails, his masculine signet ring catching the sun. 'So I asked myself why would a man, in love with girl A, marry girl B? Quite a puzzle.'

'You're imagining all this. There *is* no puzzle.'

'Yes, quite a puzzle,' he repeated softly.

'One you've been mulling over since our wedding day, I take it?' she threw at him as he watched her silently. 'Look, you're the one who's making a puzzle, as you call it, out of it, and apart from that, this hardly has anything to do with us, has it? I haven't so much as set eyes on Greg since we were married. So bang goes that theory.'

He gave a short, harsh laugh. 'Does it? I went away on business and you fly straight back here.'

'Greg is in Perth visiting his parents,' Kasey retorted. 'I told you I came to see my father.'

'Yes, so you did,' he agreed quietly, and Kasey was tight-lipped with anger as they stood glaring at each other.

Neither of them spoke, and only the cropping of the horses nearby, the rustle of the dry leaves, the distant high pitched *wit-a* of a mistletoe bird disturbed the heavy silence.

Jodan was the first to cut into the suspended stillness. 'Maybe you should give the matter some serious thought,' he said without intonation.

She blinked, not following his change in the direction of their conversation.

'The matter of a divorce,' he clarified. 'Unless you'd like to try for an annulment? But that wouldn't be strictly honest of us, would it?'

She gasped and had to resist an urge to slap his arrogant face.

'Think it over, my dear.' His inflection on the endearment mocked her. 'Now, perhaps we should be getting back.'

He untied the reins of her horse and passed them to her, his fingers not so much as glancing off hers, before he turned to mount his own borrowed mare.

They rode slowly down the hill towards the homestead, neither saying a word. How had he known about her feelings for Greg? Had she been so transparent?

Out of the corner of her eye she watched him as he moved with the horse. He was obviously no stranger to the saddle, and she wondered where and when he had acquired the skills.

How little she really knew about her husband! Kasey swallowed a faint ripple of sudden, unexpected self-pity. She might just as easily have been his secretary. Yet his private secretary would surely have seen more of him in the past month than she had. She cut off a bitter laugh. No, they were scarcely married in the accepted sense of the word. So how could there be a divorce?

A divorce. Severing the tie, a tie that had never bound them together in the beginning. It had all been a farce, from the moment he had accepted her proposal to this civilised suggestion of Jodan's that they dissolve their marriage.

A feeling of abject depression seized her in its merciless grip, and she had to fight an almost overwhelming urge to cry, to put her head down on her arms and sob out her pain. The ache seemed to have been part of her life for so long, a heavy dullness at her core, denying her any chance of the carefree happiness that had always been part of her life until everything had shattered about

her the night she'd overheard Jodan and Desiree—— No.
Ever since Greg had told her about Paula.

Then suddenly she knew that Greg and the pain she'd
felt when he had betrayed her was a mere shadow of the
agony of imagining her husband and his sister-in-law
together. But that was ludicrous. What was happening
to her?

The truth hit her like a bolt of lightning right out of
the blue. As she let her horse pick its own trail down
the hillside, she saw everything clearly for the first time.
Why she'd allowed the wedding to go ahead. Why she'd
run from Jodan at the first opportunity. She was in love
with him. And the depth of that love made her feelings
for Greg the hero-worshipping fantasy of a child by
comparison.

They dismounted at the stables, and when one of the
boys had taken their horses they turned towards the
house.

Kasey felt as though she'd been knocked out. In love
with Jodan Caine? She couldn't be! Love was a gentle...
No, that had been her adolescent fantasy. What she felt
for Jodan was neither gentle nor childish. What would
he think if he knew how much she wanted him?

Her legs felt like lead and a trickle of perspiration
picked a path between her breasts.

Now Jodan wanted a divorce. Would he change his
mind if she told him she'd fallen in love with him? Pride
took her in its grip, and she knew she could never tell
him how she felt.

Dust kicked up at every step and, tense and unsure of
herself and the situation, Kasey watched a fine film of
it cover the toes of Jodan's leather shoes. Not the most
comfortable footwear for the outback, but he seemed
unmoved by the inconvenience of the heat and dust and

the persistent fly that had him flicking his hand in front of his face.

Always controlled, was Jodan Caine, she thought wryly. Even the night he'd made love to her. Did he ever let go of that cold, steely restraint?

The sun burned brightly, fierily down on them, highlighting the slight wave in Jodan's dark hair. Irrelevantly Kasey noticed it was longer now, the shorter front strands falling forward over his brow. She also realised there were considerably more flecks of grey in the black hair over his temples, something she hadn't noticed until now. He was greying a little prematurely, for he was only thirty-five, but it somehow added to rather than detracted from his lean good looks.

She loved him.

Kasey turned her head away from her surreptitious study of her husband, her heartbeats fluctuating, and she stumbled on the gravelly ground. He made no attempt to touch her and she quickened her pace towards the house.

Her father and Jessie were on the veranda watching their approach, Mike Beazleigh smiling easily up at them, while Jessie's sharp eyes went piercingly from Kasey to Jodan.

'Caught up with her, I see.' Mike beamed at his son-in-law from his chair. 'Always did lead us a merry dance, our Kasey. I hope you keep her on a short rein.'

Kasey stiffened, treating her father to a quelling glance that broadened his grin. Jodan smiled but made no comment.

'I'll go in and change,' Kasey began coolly, but Jessie stopped her.

'You'll do no such thing! You look fine. You sit down and have this tea I've just made.' She watched as Kasey hesitated before obediently subsiding into a chair. 'Jodan's just arrived, so he won't want you rushing off,' she stated meaningfully, her eyes flicking disapprovingly to the hill behind the homestead. 'Will you, Jodan?'

'Most definitely not.'

Kasey's startled gaze flew to him in time to catch the twist of wry humour that touched his lips.

'And so it should be.' Jessie moved around to pour the tea, handing out cups to Kasey and the men before filling her own. 'Have a scone, Jodan. They're straight out of the oven.' Jessie then turned to Kasey and, when the girl refused the proffered plate, she frowned again. 'Have something to eat. You've had next to nothing all day. No wonder you're fading away to a shadow! Half a slice of toast for breakfast, little more than a few lettuce leaves for lunch.' She shook her head.

'I've never eaten a big meal, you know that, Jessie.' Kasey found herself taking a scone in desperation, biting into it, and trying valiantly to swallow it.

'Humph! You're far too thin.' Jessie sat down.

'I eat a good meal in the evening,' Kasey justified breathily, knowing all eyes were on her, sensing Jodan's cool appraisal, and wishing she could find something to say to swing the topic of conversation away from herself.

'Don't you think she's lost weight, Jodan?' Jessie persisted, turning to Kasey's husband.

Jodan raised dark, arrogant eyebrows, his cool blue eyes making another sweep of Kasey's tense body. Eventually his eyes met hers. His expression was bland, inscrutable, but she found her throat closing again, restricting her breathing.

The signs were all there, had been all along. She had always been so aware of her husband, physically aware of his proximity, the nuances of his tone, his movements.

'Come to think of it, love, you have lost weight,' her father put in. 'But you're still beautiful,' he added with a grin.

'You look drawn and pale,' Jessie continued, undaunted. 'Haven't I been saying as much this past week? And there are dark circles under your eyes.'

Her father frowned. 'You are pale, Kasey. Sure you haven't been overdoing it in the heat out here?'

Kasey laughed a little forcedly. 'Of course I haven't. I'm fine. As healthy as a horse.' In body if not in soul, she added to herself.

'That's a matter of opinion.' Jessie sipped her tea.

'Perhaps it's just reacclimatising to the dry heat after the city's humidity,' Jodan suggested, and Kasey shrugged.

'Probably.' She didn't look at him.

'You're not in the family way, are you?' Jessie demanded in her forthright manner, and Kasey almost dropped her teacup.

The older woman was fixing her with a straight stare, and Kasey's gaze shied away from the piercing eyes that had always seemed to read her like a book as she'd grown up. 'No!' she got out, feeling the flood of colour wash her face, and she shook her head emphatically. 'We've only been married for a month!'

'That doesn't seem to mean much these days.'

'Jessie!' Kasey had never been so embarrassed in her life.

'Well, it does happen, you know.' Jessie took another scone.

'Jessie, please——' Kasey began.

'Can we leave it with the assurances that we're working on it?' Jodan's deep voice startled Kasey, his words sending a shock through the entire length of her body.

What was he saying? Why prevaricate an intimacy that didn't exist when less than an hour ago he'd spoken of divorce? It would make it all the more difficult to tell her family that they were parting.

Her father was laughing, and even Jessie began to smile.

'I'm an interfering old busybody, aren't I?' Jessie softened. 'But I've been a trifle worried about Kasey since she came home. I've known her all her life and I could see something was troubling her. But now you're here, Jodan, I'm sure she'll brighten up. She was probably just missing you.'

Kasey shifted in her chair, anger overcoming her discomposure. To Jessie life was so simple. It didn't contort itself into the mess hers had become.

She had to suppress a bitter laugh. If Jessie only knew what a fiasco this conversation really was! Pregnant? Working on it? How droll of Jodan. They had shared a bed once, and she knew there had been no way she had conceived a child. There was no chance of a child for a celibate wife. Yet part of Jessie's theory had been correct. She had missed Jodan.

'Now, Jessie, enough of this,' Mike admonished the housekeeper. 'You've embarrassed the girl. All that will happen in its own good time.'

With more good timing the telephone rang, and Jessie disappeared inside to answer it, motioning Kasey back into her chair when the younger girl went to move. Kasey was forced to remain on the veranda, escape denied her once again.

Mike and Jodan began discussing the dryness of the countryside, her father shaking his head worriedly over the coming wet season and whether or not it would eventuate.

Quietly Kasey sat back, only half listening to their conversation, aware only of her tension, the unease she experienced at the deep, vibrant tone of Jodan's voice. His voice had always bothered her, unsettled her.

Jodan spoke again, moving to cross one long leg over the other, and her own body stiffened, a stab of suddenly tautened nerve-endings making her catch her breath sharply. The feelings took her aback, and she frantically forced herself to concentrate on what the men were saying.

'I was a bloody fool,' Mike was telling his son-in-law. 'Jumping down off my horse as though I were a teenager, and the next thing I knew I'd broken my leg. And I sure picked the most inconvenient time to do it, what with Peter and his wife taking the baby over to visit Sandy's parents in the States and Greg permanently over on Winterwood.'

Jodan nodded as Jessie rejoined them, a freshly brewed pot of tea in her hand.

She shook her head. 'Tsk! That was that gossip-monger Norma Main. She housekeeps for Winterwood Station next door,' she added for Jodan's benefit. 'She rang me on the pretext of checking a recipe I'd given her, but she only wanted to know if Jodan was here. Said she'd been talking to someone who'd been talking to the pilot when he called in at Heathwood Station, and he'd told them Kasey's husband had arrived.'

Jodan raised his eyebrows in surprise. 'News travels fast,' he remarked drily.

'Especially when the outback's answer to the coaxial cable gets into gear.' Mike chuckled as Jessie refilled their cups. 'That woman would be lost without her telephone.'

'I suppose it's like a lifeline out here.' Jodan took his refilled cup from Jessie. 'Something we don't often appreciate in the city.'

'And talking of the city,' Jessie put in, 'Greg and Paula arrived home from Perth this morning.'

Kasey stilled, schooling her features beneath Jessie's measured stare. She couldn't bring herself to look at Jodan.

'You may remember Greg Parker at your wedding?' Jessie turned back to Jodan and Kasey's eyelashes fluttered down to shield any expression in her eyes.

'Yes, I remember Parker.'

'Greg's like a brother to Kasey and Peter. Well,' Jessie continued, 'young Paula, his fiancée, talked Greg into getting in touch with his parents to patch up old differences. Greg hadn't seen his family in a dozen years or so, and they went over to visit them in Perth for a week.' Jessie turned to Kasey. 'Seems his parents have agreed to come to the wedding. Paula's delighted.'

Kasey knew the older woman's eyes were on her again and she made herself get slowly to her feet. 'It's getting late, and I really must have a shower and change before I give you a hand to prepare dinner.' She went to move inside.

'I wouldn't mind cleaning up myself.' Jodan stood too. 'So perhaps you could show me my room.'

Kasey glanced at Jessie, about to ask her which room she had allocated to Jodan.

'I've put Jodan in the green room,' Jessie smiled. 'And I've moved your things from your old room into the green room too, Kasey. You'll both be far more comfortable in the double bed.'

CHAPTER NINE

KASEY stopped, swinging back to face the housekeeper, her face burning. 'You shouldn't have done that, Jessie,' she began, her body tense, poised for flight, in total dismay.

How on earth was she going to get around this latest development? Everything was going crazily out of control all about her.

'Rubbish!' Jessie waved Kasey's protest aside.

'But Jodan and I—that is...' Kasey drew a quick breath. 'I haven't been sleeping very well lately and I don't want to disturb Jodan.'

'You always slept like a log,' Jessie commented accusingly.

'Mostly I do, but——' Kasey's eyes widened as Jodan stepped forward.

'The green room will be fine, Jessie,' he said easily. 'Kasey's too solicitous. She tries to spoil me.' His bland gaze met Kasey's and he smiled. 'She knows I don't mind being disturbed.'

Kasey couldn't have spoken if her life depended on it. His undeniably sensual smile took her breath away while his words, the slightly lowered, intimate intonation, started a deep fire inside her that threatened to blaze out of hand. It would be so easy to relax her control, let go, indulge in the promise he was offering. Pretend. Could she...?

Jessie was beaming. 'And apart from that I didn't want you waking me up in the middle of the night stumbling back and forth, now did I?'

Jodan laughed, as naturally as any man would at the connotation in Jessie's teasing words, and he moved to take Kasey's arm. 'Kasey can show me the way to our room.'

The slight pressure of his fingers pulled her out of her shocked immobility and she stepped through the open double doors, her face suddenly aflame again. Jodan let her go when they were out of sight of her father and Jessie, and Kasey had to restrain herself from rubbing her arm where his fingers had touched her bare skin. It seemed to be tingling, burning.

Why are you here, Jodan? she wanted to scream at him. Now it was all so complicated.

'I'm sorry.' She was amazed at the flat evenness of her voice. 'I didn't even think about——' She stopped and made a futile gesture with her hands.

'About the sleeping arrangements,' he finished with equal formality. 'It's only natural they'd expect us to share a bed,' he said casually, as though he was discussing the weather.

Perhaps it meant as much as the weather to him. How she wished she could be as nonchalant! 'But what are we going to do about it?' Kasey threw open the door of the green room and stepped inside.

The bedroom was large, and high double doors opened out on to the wide, covered veranda. This was typical of all the bedrooms, and the doors were rarely closed day or night.

Two huge old cedar wardrobes stood along one wall, and Kasey absently registered the smell of Jessie's furniture polish and the clean freshness of the pervading outdoors, dry grass, eucalypts.

Behind them was a large matching cedar dressing-table, the brass handles on the drawers gleaming. The rectangular mirror attached to the top of the dressing-table reflected the framed picture of the huge cedar double bed, its white crocheted bedspread blending in so well with the solid old furniture. The bed looked soft and welcoming.

This room, high-ceilinged and painted in a very pale apple-green, was so vastly different from Kasey's bedroom in Jodan's apartment in the city. But at least that room in the city came without Jodan Caine.

She closed her eyes to blot out the beckoning comfort of the bed and then, in control, turned back to face her husband.

He was unbuttoning his shirt, the whiteness of the material in stark contrast to the tanned expanse of hard flesh taut across his chest.

'What are you doing?' she demanded, agitation thinning her voice.

'I need a shower, and I usually remove my clothes to do that,' he said wryly. 'I suppose the bathroom's next door.'

'Yes. But you can't—I mean, we can't——'

Jodan pulled his shirt from the waistband of his trousers, slid his arms from the sleeves and tossed the garment on to the chair by the door.

Like moths to a flame, Kasey's eyes were drawn to the breadth of his shoulders, the firm, tapering midriff. He was nicely proportioned, not overly muscular. He'd told her he usually jogged a couple of times a week, time permitting.

For one so dark, he didn't have a lot of body hair, but on his chest there was a sparse mat of fine dark curls that arrowed downwards.

Her mouth went suddenly dry and she moistened her lips with her tongue-tip. She was almost overcome by a purely sexual urge to close the physical space between them, reach out her hand in invitation, feel his firm flesh, the dark whorls of hair. Dismay clutched at her.

'I wasn't about to suggest we shower together,' he remarked, misconstruing the expression on her pale face. He crossed to the nearest wardrobe and opened the door, taking out one of his fresh shirts which Jessie had unpacked and hung there.

Kasey watched him speechlessly, mesmerised by the ripple of masculine muscle across his back.

'Or has that been our trouble, Kasey? Should we have showered together in the beginning, I wonder?' He turned back to face her, casting the shirt over the end of the bed.

She felt herself flush. He was playing with her, she could see that in his eyes, a watchful, teasing brightness lightening their cold blueness.

'We could remedy that,' he said softly.

'Don't be ridiculous!' Kasey folded her arms defensively as his eyes dropped to slide down over her plain shirt, her faded jeans. 'I'll use my own bathroom—and don't worry, I'll be sleeping in my old room.' She turned away.

'Kasey!' His voice stopped her.

'Unless you want to have to fend off more to-the-point questions from Jessie, I suggest you sleep in here where she's put you.'

'But where will you sleep?' she stammered.

'In here too.'

'I can't sleep——'

'For heaven's sake!' He moved irritatedly. 'You'll be safe enough.' He threw the words at her. 'I assure you I don't intend to force myself on you.' His gaze held hers relentlessly.

'I didn't say you—well, that you would,' Kasey managed to get out, thrusting her clenched hands into the pockets of her jeans, memories of their wedding night playing vividly in her mind.

'OK, we've settled that. So let's be civilised adults about it, shall we?' He walked towards her, his hand unbuckling his belt, and Kasey turned and fled.

'Civilised adults!' Kasey muttered the words angrily as she stood beneath the cool shower spray. She felt more like a nervous adolescent. Jodan might be used to sharing his bed with a string of women, but she'd slept alone, including during the weeks of her marriage. Apart from that first disastrous night, her wedding night.

She closed her eyes, running the shower over her face, and her mind produced a vision, a disturbing picture in full colour of Jodan, his long, naked body sliding into the bed beside her. She stood motionless, her body tingling.

Should we shower together? he'd asked. At that moment she almost felt his hands, soapy-smooth, gliding over her skin. Her soft, aroused moan brought her to her senses with sudden shock.

She had to be mad! The heat out here was getting to her. Angry with herself, she switched off the shower and all but sprang from the cubicle. Reaching for a fluffy blue bath sheet, she began towelling herself dry with unnecessary vigour.

Kasey slipped into a pair of pale khaki knee-length shorts and a matching khaki and white striped shirt. With her feet bare, she strolled out of the door of what had been her old bedroom, on to the wide veranda on the southern side of the house. She rested her cheek against the familiar warmth of the veranda post and sighed.

Only a month ago she'd thought she would never recover from the pain, the hurt Greg had caused her. But of course life had gone on, regardless. That night, the night Greg had called at her flat, had set her on the path to this disastrous marriage between herself and Jodan Caine.

One mistake on top of another. Was she destined to flounder through life making one monumental blunder after another? What was she to do?

'Hello, Kasey.'

The sound of her name made her jump and she straightened, turning towards the man seated astride the black gelding.

'Sorry I startled you. I thought you saw me coming.'

'No—it's all right. I must have been daydreaming.' She swallowed. 'How are you, Greg?'

He shrugged. 'OK.' He was watching her a little guardedly. 'You look well,' he added, pulling on the reins of his horse as it took a side-step. 'City life seems to be agreeing with you.'

Kasey inclined her head. Greg obviously wasn't seeing the strain that Jessie kept referring to at length. 'Perhaps it's married life,' she quipped, then felt just a little guilty as his lips tightened. 'And talking of married life, how are the plans for your wedding coming along?'

'Fine,' he replied flatly. 'Paula's done all that. I'm not up on all the female ballyhoo that goes with it. I'd rather just sign the papers, but Paula wants all the trimmings.'

Kasey allowed her gaze to roam his face. A tuft of damp blond hair escaped from beneath his hat, and there were fine lines radiating out from the corners of his blue eyes. Had he always had that petulant, dissatisfied droop to his lips? Could he be unhappy?

If he was it was of his own making, she told herself. Greg had made his choice, and now it was far too late to change his mind.

Her eyes went to him again. That night in her flat when they'd almost made love—did he remember that? She felt a soft flush touch her cheeks and she straightened.

'How's Mike?' he asked.

'He's fine, but frustrated at being housebound.' This was safer ground. 'He's around on the front veranda if you want to see him.'

He coloured slightly. 'Actually, I came to see you.' He swung down from his horse, tethered the animal in the shade of a tree and hooked his hat over the pommel. As he climbed the steps towards her he ran his fingers through the damp strands of his hair. He stopped one step from the top, only a foot or two from her. 'Norma Main said you arrived the day after we left for Perth.

Kasey stepped back from him, casually leaning back against the railing. 'Yes. Jessie tells me you went to Perth to see your parents.'

He nodded. 'Paula set it up.'

'Were they pleased to see you?' Kasey mouthed the words, mere conversation, as she tried to analyse her feelings for the man who had meant so much to her. Her first love. They had ridden together, cleaned the stables together, swum in the waterhole together. Yet she seemed unable to bring the two of them into any perspective. The past, their past, was out of focus.

'I guess so. Mum was, anyway. It was a bit strained at first, but things settled down. We made our peace.'

'I'm glad,' Kasey told him honestly.

Greg nodded. 'It was good to see my brother again. He's married too, has three kids.' He paused. 'They all thought Paula was tops.' His eyes were watching her, and she realised he was seeking some response. That she was jealous?

His probe was quite deliberate, and under other circumstances Kasey knew she would have been cut to the quick. How could he do that?

Her eyes reassessed him and for the first time she noticed the immaturity, the weakness she'd thought was boyish charm. The hero she'd worshipped for years. How could she have been so wrong?

Greg's fair good looks, his boyishness, seemed somehow insipid compared to the hard, masculine strength that sat so naturally on Jodan. Greg was certainly good-looking, but—— Jodan. It always came back to Jodan. Yet if it hadn't been for Greg she would never have married him.

And on Saturday Greg would be marrying Paula. Kasey had accepted the invitation to attend, and now she couldn't care less if she put in an appearance or not, couldn't care if she saved face in front of her family and friends with her tall, handsome husband by her side.

'She made quite a hit with my father,' Greg was saying, still watching her face.

'Paula's a nice girl,' she said, and knew it was true.

Greg's eyes met hers. 'Akoonah Downs hasn't been the same without you,' he said softly.

Kasey made herself laugh lightly. 'Jessie tells me they haven't seen much of you. From what I hear you've had your hands full on Winterwood now that you've taken over.'

'Henry's pretty much crippled with arthritis, so...' He shrugged, and silence fell between them.

So you've got what you wanted, Greg, your own station, Kasey wanted to say, but couldn't.

'I didn't come over here because it hardly seemed worth it when you weren't here.' He shifted, and rested his hand on the railing mere inches from Kasey's. 'I've missed you.'

'I've been away before for longer periods than this,' Kasey reminded him, 'when I was at school and college.'

'That was different.' His fingers slid over hers, held them captive on the rail beneath his.

'Greg!' Kasey tried to draw her hand away, but he held her fast.

'Have you missed me, Kasey?' he asked, a note of pleading in his tone. 'Like I've missed you?'

But before Kasey could utter a sound a deep voice sliced between them.

'Ah, here you are, darling.' Jodan stepped through the open door.

Both Greg and Kasey sprang guiltily backwards, Greg releasing Kasey's hand as though it suddenly burned him. In two unhurried strides Jodan was beside her, one arm going oh, so casually around her, his fingers at her waist.

'Parker, isn't it?' Jodan's tone was just short of rude, and Greg's body tensed, his lips thinning.

'Greg Parker,' he bit out between his teeth.

'You've taken over Winterwood Station, I believe,' Jodan remarked easily, his hand exerting a slight pressure, bringing Kasey closer to him, his fingers now resting intimately just below the mound of her breast.

'You met Greg on our wedding day,' Kasey put in quickly, unable to move from his firm grip.

'Mmm!' Jodan's other hand came around her so that she was completely encircled in his arms now, and she could feel his breath gently stirring her hair. Her heart had jumped into her mouth, thumping loudly. 'I vaguely remember the introduction, but you'll understand, Parker, I had other things on my mind that day.' His lips nuzzled the curve of Kasey's neck.

'I should go and see Mike.' Greg's eyes moved icily over Kasey as she stood in her husband's arms.

'Jessie's just brewed another cup of tea,' Jodan told them lightly. 'And I was sent to round Kasey up.'

'I don't think Jessie meant literally!' Kasey forced a laugh and tried to unwind Jodan's arms. He held her fast.

'Go on around, Parker.' He dismissed the other man. 'We'll join you in a few moments.' His smile suggested that he intended to steal a few moments with his wife.

Without a word, Greg strode down the veranda and around the corner of the house, his boots beating an angry tattoo on the loose wooden boards.

Jodan slowly released her, but his hard body barred her way. 'Don't play me for a fool, Kasey,' he growled softly.

'I don't know what you mean,' Kasey said with as much conviction as she could, and that wasn't much, she had to admit. He'd obviously seen Greg clutching her hand.

'You're my wife, and until I say so that's the way it stays. Any differences we have stay private. Do I make myself clear?'

'You're being ridiculous——'

'Ridiculous or not, you'd be advised to do as I say,' he broke in on her. 'And that includes not sharing romantic interludes with that pretty boy Parker.'

'I wasn't sharing a romantic interlude with Greg!' Kasey's own anger began to boil. 'We were simply talking.'

'Holding hands while you did so.' Jodan gave a harsh laugh. 'How nice!'

'If you're not careful, Jodan, I'll think you're jealous,' she taunted, and his hand reached out, clasped her arm, his fingers biting into her flesh.

His lips compressed as his jaw tightened, and he looked as though he'd like to strangle her right there and then. But he seemed to take hold of himself, controlling his obvious rage.

'Don't push me, Kasey, because we both know you'll be biting off far more than you can chew. Just keep away from Parker.' The pressure of his fingers on her arm relaxed a little and he started walking after Greg. 'Let's join the others, shall we?'

Jessie was passing Greg a plate when Kasey and Jodan approached.

'My favourite date loaf,' said Greg, over-brightly. 'You must have known I was coming, Jessie.'

'I was sure you would,' the older woman remarked drily, and began to fill cups for Jodan and Kasey.

Kasey subsided weakly into a chair, her heartbeats still racing from her encounter with her husband. And when he shifted his own chair so that his long leg lightly rested against hers, she was sure everyone would hear their thunderous pounding. She slid a glance at him.

He was watching her, his cool blue eyes alert beneath shuttered lids. His gaze moved almost indolently to Greg and then back to her.

Have you missed me, Kasey? Like I've missed you?

Had Jodan overheard Greg's impassioned words? He must have. Otherwise why the pretentious display of husbandly possession, holding her in his arms, play-acting a part? And his despicable ultimatum afterwards.

'How's Paula?' Jessie was asking Greg as he bit into his second slice of date loaf. 'Everything fixed up ready for the wedding?'

Greg nodded. 'She's fine, and as far as I know everything's arranged.'

Kasey glanced at him sharply. And that was as much as he cared, by the sound of it. Poor Paula!

'How are the levels in the dam?' Greg changed the subject, turning to Mike.

They fell to discussing the usual subjects, and Kasey noticed that Jodan seemed content to listen. Which was more than she was capable of. He'd shifted his weight and now rested his hand on her thigh, fingers moving in an almost abstracted caress that was having a totally unnerving effect on her.

When Jessie stood up to start the evening meal, Kasey eagerly offered to help her with the preparations.

'Will Jodan be staying until the weekend for Greg's wedding?' Jessie asked as she kneaded the pastry for the steak and kidney pie she was making for dinner.

'I don't know.' Kasey tried to keep her voice even. 'He didn't ... we didn't discuss it.' She frowned unconsciously. 'I shouldn't think so. He won't be able to spare much time away from the business. It's been pretty hectic these past few weeks since his brother's heart attack.'

Jessie watched the younger woman as she shelled the peas picked fresh from the garden Jessie tended so lovingly in the almost impossible heat. Aware of Jessie's scrutiny, Kasey's fingers fumbled and she dropped a couple of peas on the floor. She bent down to retrieve them, grateful for the excuse to hide the colour in her cheeks.

'And you'll be going back with him.' It was a statement.

'No, I'll stay on a while,' Kasey said evenly.

Jessie had paused with her floury hands in the dough. 'Is there something wrong between you two?' she asked levelly, and Kasey forced herself to look up in surprise.

'Wrong? Of course not. What could be wrong?'

'Is that why you're here? Why he came after you?'

Kasey made herself laugh. 'Jessie, really! I came home because of Dad's accident and to see you both. That's not hard to believe, is it?'

'I suppose not,' Jessie agreed grudgingly. 'But you're not yourself, not by a long chalk. You're not the Kasey who left here.'

'I hope not. I'm all grown-up now, Jessie, a sober married woman, and—well, perhaps some of the city has rubbed off on me.'

'Cities! Stifling places, if you ask me.'

Kasey almost sighed with relief as Jessie became side-tracked.

'Can't abide cities myself—never could. All those dangerous vehicles, and the fumes! I warned young Paula to be careful before Greg took her over to Perth. And speaking of Greg...'

Kasey tensed, waiting for Jessie's next words, pre-pared to cut the housekeeper off, but as usual Jessie always said what she wanted to say.

'He thinks he's still in love with you.'

'Oh, Jessie——!'

'Don't "oh, Jessie" me! You know what I mean, and I know you won't encourage him, Kasey.' Jessie sighed. 'Try not to worry about it, love—he'll get over it. Greg's a butterfly and still immature, regardless of the fact that he's old enough to know better. He fancies having something that's unattainable, but once he's married to Paula he'll settle down, you'll see.'

'Will he be happy, do you think?' Kasey asked pensively.

'I'm sure he will,' Jessie reassured her. 'Paula worships him, and he'll be King of Winterwood rather than second fiddle here on Akoonah Downs.'

Kasey's eyes widened in dismay. How could Jessie know——?

She nodded. 'I've known how Greg thinks for years, love, and so has your father. That's why he never made a fuss about your crush on Greg. He knew it wouldn't be enough for Greg.'

Kasey sighed. Everyone had known except her.

'Your father's just happy to see you settled with someone as nice as Jodan.' Jessie smiled. 'And so am I. Now, let's get this meal into gear.'

Surprisingly, the meal that night passed easily enough. If Jodan was deliberately setting out to charm Kasey's family, he was succeeding admirably.

From beneath her lashes Kasey watched him, as he gently teased Jessie until the woman's thin, weathered face was aglow, as he set her father laughing with his anecdotes on the vagaries of computers and their keepers.

With dinner behind them they retired to the living-room, and after about an hour Kasey had to stifle her yawns. She was tired and emotionally drained. But should she excuse herself first, and thus try to be asleep before Jodan joined her? Or should she wait until he was asleep and then go to bed herself?

Then she realised everyone was looking at her. 'I'm sorry. Did I miss something?' she apologised.

Jodan got to his feet. 'You look half asleep,' he said easily, and flexed his back muscles. 'I'm tired myself, I have to admit. An early night will do us both good. Would you excuse us, Mike?'

Kasey's father nodded. 'We keep early hours out here anyway. I won't be long out of bed myself.'

'I'll make some tea if you like, Dad,' Kasey suggested in a rush.

'None for me, love,' Mike refused. 'You get off to bed now. Jodan's right—you look like you're asleep on your feet.' He winked at her and she flushed hotly as she stood in the middle of the floor, a mass of indecision. She couldn't go with Jodan.

He crossed the floor and caringly took her arm. 'Off to bed with you. 'Night, Mike—Jessie.'

Before Kasey had a chance to protest she found herself in the hallway, on the way to their room.

Her step faltered. 'Look, I'll leave you to an undisturbed night. No one will know if I slip along to my room.'

They had reached the green room now and Jodan thrust her inside, reaching around to flick on the light.

'I thought we'd settled this.' He frowned exasperatedly.

'I really don't think we have to explain our sleeping arrangements to anyone, Jodan. Who cares, anyway?'

'I do. Jessie loves to chatter, and I don't want my private life bandied about the outback from here to back of Bourke.'

'There are no scandal-sheet spies out here, Jodan,' she said sarcastically, and hurried on at his set expression, 'And besides, if we decide to——' Kasey stopped, her eyes coming to rest on the small pulse that was beating in his tense jaw. His eyes also reflected his anger, and her voice faded.

'To what?'

'You mentioned a divorce this morning,' she got out.

'We aren't divorced yet.' He drew his shirt over his head. 'Until then I don't care to have any speculation about our private life.'

'I can't see how it matters out here. Akoonah Downs isn't exactly at the centre of the social hub,' Kasey appealed to him.

He shrugged, and the overhead light sent flashes of silver through his dark hair. 'Would your father and Jessie understand our preference for separate beds?'

Kasey paused.

'I rest my case. Now, I'll take a turn around the veranda while you change, to save us getting into another debate on that subject.' Without waiting for her comment, he strolled through the open doors and into the semi-darkness.

Kasey stood where he had left her, her eyes drawn to the large bed. Surely the width of it, the equivalent of a modern queen-size, would mean plenty of space, so they needn't even touch. She shivered.

Stepping across to the bed, she saw that Jessie had turned down the spread and set out her best satin nightdress. Kasey clutched the soft folds, then rolled the garment up, pushing it into the top drawer of the dressing-table and rummaging around until she found the faded oversized T-shirt she usually slept in. Hurriedly she shed her clothes and pulled the T-shirt over her head.

She spared a quick glance at her reflection in the mirror. The baggy nightshirt to some extent disguised her figure, although the neckline had stretched out of shape and revealed the beginnings of the creamy mounds of her breasts. Adjusting the shoulders, she turned and climbed beneath the clean, fresh sheets.

As if on cue, Jodan reappeared. His gaze barely flicked over her before he kicked off his shoes and began to unzip his trousers.

'You can't undress in here!' The words burst forth before Kasey could draw them back.

He paused. 'Why not?' One eyebrow quirked.

'Well, because——'

He slipped the material over his hips, and stood before her wearing only a pair of very brief underpants which left little to the imagination.

As she watched, dry-mouthed now, her heartbeats beginning to race, he strode towards the bed.

'You can't mean to sleep in just those—those——'

'No, I don't mean to sleep in just these,' he mocked. 'As a matter of fact, I sleep *au naturel*, as I think you already know.' And with that he discarded his last piece of clothing.

Red-faced, Kasey turned away, tensing as the bed moved as he climbed beneath the sheet.

'I do believe you're blushing, my dear. Such a virginal display! Just a little out of date in this day and age, don't you think?'

For some seconds Kasey was stunned by his taunts, shocked at his sarcastic arrogance. And there was that funny shaft of pain in her chest. Virginal. He'd been the one to change all that. She caught her bottom lip between her teeth. How could he? Her anger started to rise.

His eyes had narrowed, but she caught the cold glint of them between his lids and his lips twisted derisively. 'That wasn't what I meant, Kasey, and I think you know that.'

'No, I don't know that, and it sounded like it from here,' she flung at him. Her nervous indignation now had her in its grip. 'What an amazing penchant for justification men seem to have!'

'I meant we'd shared a bed before,' he put in firmly.

'Which wasn't exactly my idea——'

'Kasey, I'm tired——'

'So am I—of this one-sided marriage. It's always what *you* want. The great Jodan Caine!'

He sat up with one lithe movement, the sheet slipping low on his hips. 'If you're spoiling for a fight, Kasey, I'd appreciate it if you'd leave it until some other time. I've had one hell of a day, what with one thing and another.'

'And if I don't choose to follow my master's wishes?' Kasey made a mocking inclination of her head.

'Then your master may find a particularly distasteful method of drawing the evening to a close.' His eyes met, challenged hers, and Kasey's gaze flickered and fell, all bravado leaving her.

'You wouldn't!'

CHAPTER TEN

'WOULDN'T I?' Jodan's hand came out to Kasey and he slowly let his fingertip move downwards over her ear to the low neckline of her nightshirt.

Colour flooded her face and she recoiled. But not before her traitorous senses had gone mad at that feather-soft, sensuous touch.

He held her gaze for earth-stopping moments. 'We both need some sleep, Kasey, don't you think?'

With that he rolled away from her and settled on his side of the bed.

The night stretched ahead into eternity as she lay sleepless, stiff and tense beside the relaxed and slumbering form of her husband. Her stomach churned as she relived their altercation and then her imagination took over, playing the alternative ending had she continued to challenge him. That only served to agitate her even more.

Would he have carried out that arrogantly delivered threat? Well, she'd never know now. But she firmly believed he would be ruthless enough to use whatever means he could to get his way.

Damn him! He was an arrogant, overbearing, presumptuous... her fingers tightened on the sheet she still clutched to her chin...attractive, magnetic, exciting and totally desirable man.

Kasey almost groaned aloud. How she wanted him to make love to her! And how she wished she had the courage to turn to him, waken him and show him. But of course, she couldn't do that. Could she? No! Resolutely she closed her eyes and willed the oblivion of sleep.

At some stage she must have dozed off, for the room had just begun to lighten when she stirred with the feeling that something, some sound, had awoken her. She opened her eyes, listening.

'Kasey.'

The thick muttered sound of her name had her stiffening uneasily on her edge of the bed.

'Kasey,' Jodan repeated, moving restlessly.

What did he want? Was he ill?

He shifted again, turning over, his arm reaching out, encountering hers.

'What . . . what is it?' she asked breathily.

'Kasey.' He murmured something unintelligible, and then, 'Don't go. Don't go.'

Kasey raised herself on one elbow, peering down at him in the semi-darkness, realising he was asleep and dreaming.

'Don't go.' He was closer now and his arm imprisoned her, lying heavily across her midriff as she sank back on to the bed.

She drew a ragged breath and gently tried to lift the dead weight of his arm. This seemed to distress him and he muttered again, pulling her close to him. Her old T-shirt stretched and twisted, the neckline slipping over her shoulder, and his mouth now rested there against her bare skin.

His lips stirred, titillated that over-sensitised skin, and Kasey froze. What should she do? Should she wake him? Or try to leave the bed herself?

His arm about her tightened, his lips now nuzzling the curve of her neck, and, as much as Kasey tried to remain immune to his nearness, the now familiar ache in the pit of her stomach began to spread through her body.

His teeth nibbled her earlobe and she shivered, the breath she was holding escaping in a sharp sigh. Then his mouth moved downwards to settle on the spot at the base of her throat where her pulse throbbed, raced. Desire tore through her like wildfire and before she knew what she was about her fingers were gently, ever so softly tracing the hard muscle of his upper arm.

It was as though she stood apart from herself, watching, watched as those fingers travelled upwards over his shoulder to his ear, lingered there, one fingertip tracing its contours, moved across to smooth the light furrow on his wide brow, meandered down his cheek, along the line of his jaw, feeling the fine bristles, climbed again to describe his straight nose, paused, then, drawn like a moth to a flame, softly touched his lips.

They were firm, perfectly shaped, their outline distinctly defined. She gently touched first the top lip and then the fuller bottom one, and suddenly her finger was in his mouth, and his tongue teased its tip.

Kasey's gaze darted in surprise from its fascinated scrutiny of his lips to meet his eyes. They were open now, alert, and, in the dusky glow of daybreak, held hers. The fire that raced through her was reflected in their blue, black-lashed depths. Dark, burning blue. How could she ever have imagined his eyes were cold?

His arm that still held her captive moved slowly, his hand going to the curve of her throat, trailed down, tugging the loose T-shirt with it, until one creamy breast was free. His fingers slowly circled, climbed, taking forever, or so it seemed to Kasey, to reach the peak, now rigid and aroused.

Yet still his eyes relentlessly held hers.

Kasey moaned softly, an abandoned, wanton sound she scarcely recognised as her own voice.

'Jodan, please!' Please stop or please don't stop? She was far beyond rational thought. It was as though she'd been primed, held waiting, and one touch, Jodan's touch, was the spark to her tinder-dry thirst that set her raging, aflame.

He shifted his weight, threw back the sheet and deftly removed her T-shirt, so that she lay before him naked apart from her bikini pants, the soft dawn light cascading through the open doors to bathe her skin.

'Beautiful,' he murmured huskily, 'so beautiful.' Lowering his head, he nuzzled each breast, his lips leaving soft, light kisses over her midriff, her waist, his tongue-tip teasing impossibly every aching square inch.

Just as easily he dispensed with her panties and his hand slid downwards, his fingers finding every secret, responsive place. Kasey caught her breath, not daring to believe he could make her feel this way.

Her fingers began their own exploration, each curve of his muscular body, the smooth indentation of his backbone, lower over the taut mound of his buttocks. Her lips tasted the warm skin of his shoulder, his chest, his small, tense male nipples. She gasped, feeling she could lose herself in his heady, masculine perfume. His skin was warm and silken to her touch and he moaned softly, deep in his throat, as her caresses became more assured. Then his lips claimed hers.

Unashamedly she arched to meet him, clasping his body to hers, craving, aching for fulfilment. Jodan moved his long body over hers and she caught her breath in sudden apprehension.

His deep voice murmured against her, unintelligible words but softly soothing, his fingers fanning the flame of desire until she knew only that she wanted him to assuage this burning need that overrode her fears. She met his passion with her own, took pleasure from him and gave it, until they both collapsed exhausted on to the bed.

Surprisingly Kasey drifted off to sleep almost immediately, her body sated, safely cocooned in Jodan's arms. It had been so wonderful, nothing like the first time, and she knew a smile lingered on her face as Jodan held her close in the circle of his arms.

When she awoke the sun was streaming into the room and Jodan was standing before the mirror, his back to her, combing his dark hair. He'd obviously just showered, for his hair was still damp and the musky scent of his shaving-lotion wafted across the room to her. Even as she watched him, her eyes drinking in the long, hard length of him, she felt the faint stirring of wanting in the pit of her stomach.

Had she really behaved so recklessly, so unrestrainedly, just a few short hours ago? It was unbelievable. Perhaps she had dreamed it . . .? But no, it had been real enough. She made a tentative movement, stretching her slightly stiff muscles that were proof, if she needed it, of their lovemaking.

She must have made some sound, for Jodan turned, his brush still in his hand, a slightly wary expression on his face.

Only then did the full extent of her actions really hit her, and a heavy coldness gripped her. Had she actually invited his possession? Begged him to make love to her? She rather feared she had. Colour suffused her face and she pulled the sheet defensively over her nakedness.

A shutter fell over Jodan's face and he slowly replaced the hairbrush on the dressing-table. 'Good morning,' he said evenly.

Kasey's eyes widened, her breath escaping in a soft rush. How prosaic! He could act so normally after what they'd done. Because it's not a novelty to him, a little voice reminded her. He was hardly the blushing little novice she was.

'I'll leave you to dress. Jessie has breakfast ready.' He walked to the door, paused, half turned back to her and then silently left her, quietly closing the door behind him.

Kasey blinked at the closed door. This must have been just a crazy hallucination, a wildly erotic dream. Her fingers found her bruised lips and she gave a low moan of pain that had nothing to do with her physical being.

She pushed herself into a sitting position, flushing at the sight of the pale bruise on her left breast, and a hot wave of humiliation rose to taunt her. Angry at herself, she jumped up and pulled on her robe. Quickly she straightened and made the bed, wishing as she did so that she could as quickly wipe her memories from her mind. 'Fat chance,' she muttered aloud as she gathered her clothes and headed down the passage to the shower.

When she joined the others on the veranda she chose a chair as far away from her husband as possible, and she couldn't bring herself to look at him.

'Why don't you take Jodan out to the swimming-hole, love? Show him it's not all dust and flies out here on the Downs,' her father suggested after Kasey had somehow forced down a slice of toast and a cup of coffee.

She flicked a glance at Jodan's profile. 'It's rather hot for riding,' she began.

'Take the jeep,' Mike countered. 'You can drive just about up to the pool with the four-wheel-drive.'

'It's still rather a long walk.'

'A short stroll, you mean.' Mike laughed.

'But you'll be needing the jeep to drive out to the air-strip to collect the tractor parts you said were being flown in today,' Kasey reminded him.

'That's only a couple of cartons. Billy can take the utility.' He waved a hand dismissively and turned to his son-in-law. 'I can assure you the short walk up to the pool is well worth it, Jodan. A cool oasis in the desert, is the old swimming-hole.'

'I'd like to see it,' Jodan said evenly, 'but I'd prefer to go on horseback. I don't get the time or opportunity in the city to keep up my riding skills.'

'Well, there you are.' Mike grinned triumphantly at his daughter. 'Give Billy a ring down at the stables and ask him to saddle up ready for you.'

'I'll do that.' Jessie beamed as she topped up everyone's cups of coffee. 'You'll be surprised how beautiful the area is, Jodan. Kasey and the boys lived at the pool when they were youngsters.' She chuckled. 'Remember the afternoon you hid the boys' clothes and then left them to it? And all because they wouldn't take you with them to the dance! Peter was so angry with you he wouldn't talk to you for days, but Greg thought it was the joke of the century.'

'We should be making a move if we're going.' Kasey stood up. Jessie's reminiscences were all she needed just at the moment. 'I'll go and change into my jeans.'

'Don't forget your swimsuit!' Jessie called after her.

How was she going to get through the next few hours alone with Jodan? To take him to the pool would be torture. It was a special place for her. And she wanted it to be a special place for him, her husband, the man she loved.

If they'd had a proper marriage, if they'd met, fallen in love, she would have jumped at the chance to be alone with him there, to share with him the place where she'd dreamed her girlish dreams. As a teenager she'd often lain stretched out on the flat rock overlooking the pool a dozen feet below, so cool, gazing up at the patches of clear blue sky through the canopy of leaves. Greg, she reminded herself, her dreams had been of Greg.

Those dreams had been the sweet fantasies of youth. Now she'd grown up, seen through the wash of perfection she'd painted over Greg. Now she knew her real-life dream. Loving Jodan, being loved by him.

A painful lump of unshed tears swelled in her throat. Half a dream, Kasey, she told herself on a wave of self-pity. Jodan wasn't in love with her. He wanted a divorce. What a fool she had been to allow herself to fall in love with him!

She zipped her jeans and slowly crossed to the door. Was Jodan dreading the next few hours as much as she was?

She walked down the hall and stepped out on to the veranda just as Jodan rounded the corner of the house. Kasey stopped, watched as he approached, his long legs covering the distance separating them in easy, unhurried strides.

'Billy hasn't brought the horses up yet,' she said inanely.

'So I see.' He raised one sardonic dark eyebrow, and Kasey shoved her shaking hands into the pockets of her jeans. 'We can ride off in different directions if you like,' he added flatly.

Kasey's eyes flashed to his and away again. 'I don't know what you mean.'

'Sure you do. You have a very transparent face, my dear. It tells me you'd rather walk over a bed of hot coals than go riding with me.'

'Oh, Jodan, that's——'

His soft bitter laugh cut her off. 'And talking of beds, we're down to the basis there, aren't we?'

Kasey flushed a deep scarlet.

'Ever since you left our marriage bed this morning you've been so studiously forgetting we were ever there together.'

He stood before her, legs planted apart, hands resting firmly on his hips. And she felt his cold blue gaze dissecting her.

'I'm afraid it happened, Kasey. You can't pretend it didn't by not mentioning it, by not even registering the fact that I'm here.'

'Jodan, really! You're being...' Kasey sought the right words.

'Honest,' he finished evenly. 'We slept together. We made love together—the two of us, you and me. And we both enjoyed it.' He took a step closer to her. 'We *did* enjoy it, didn't we, Kasey?'

When she made no reply he expelled a long, disgusted breath. 'I'm not a callow youth, Kasey. I do know when a woman's enjoying being made love to, and when she isn't. Last night you were not faking your responses.'

'I didn't say I was—that I didn't,' Kasey said breathlessly.

She made herself move then, crossing the few steps to the railing, hands clutching its solidness for support. Did he realise the effect his softly spoken words were having on her, the memories he was evoking? She could almost feel his hands, his lips on her skin. If he looked into her eyes he'd see the truth reflected there. That she wished they were back in that huge bed together, the two of them—making love.

'So now,' Jodan continued wryly, 'I suppose you're going to demand an apology. I was the one who assured you that you were safe from me, wasn't I? So therefore I must have taken advantage of you.'

'Jodan, I can't see why we have to—to hold this—this post-mortem.' Kasey stumbled over her words. 'Wouldn't it be better if we both just tried to forget it happened?'

There was a heavy, deafening silence when even the hot breeze seemed to hold its breath. Then his fingers closed on her arm, swinging her back to face him. 'Forget it happened? Can you, Kasey?' he got out through lips that were thin and tight. 'Can you forget it happened?'

She tried to shrug. 'Of course.' Her voice didn't sound like her own and she kept her eyes on the top button of his shirt, tried to convince herself she believed what she said was true, tried to keep the thoughts of his hard, tanned flesh beneath the shirt from her mind. But she failed.

'Are you taking precautions?' he asked baldly, and her eyes rose in shocked surprise.

Her mouth went dry. She tried to speak, but no words came and she could only shake her head negatingly.

Something flickered in the cold expression in his eyes. 'Well, I'm afraid I didn't come prepared either.'

'That . . . that doesn't mean I . . . I have to be . . .' Kasey swallowed. 'It's not likely.'

He smiled, a cold, tense movement of his lips. 'Famous last words, my dear.'

A million crazy thoughts ricocheted around inside her. She even dared hope . . . But she was being ridiculous. She didn't want to hold him that way. She wanted more.

'Jodan, this is . . . Oh, for heaven's sake, I don't want to talk about it! You have my word I'm not going to hold anything over you or contest your divorce. Last night was just a mistake.'

His fingers still held her arm, burned through the thin cotton of her shirt, tightened momentarily before setting her free. 'My mistake,' he said bitterly, and gave an equally bitter, harsh laugh, his eyelashes shielding his expression. 'My biggest mistake,' he repeated softly, so quietly she barely heard the words.

And those words cut her to the bone. He was admitting that last night had been an unfortunate lapse on his part that should never have happened. All a mistake. Like their marriage.

She made herself move away from him, away from the heady enervation of his nearness, and she forced herself to gather together some of the tattered remnants of her pride.

'There's no need to keep blaming yourself, Jodan. The mistake was mine. I'm the one who——' she swallowed '—who... I instigated the... You were asleep, dreaming, and I was the one who—who seduced you.'

His lips twisted self-derisively. 'That's quite magnanimous of you to make such an admission, but I'm afraid you couldn't have seduced——' he grimaced '—me if I'd been unwilling.'

Before Kasey could comment, Billy Saturday came around the corner of the house leading two horses, both saddled and ready.

'You goin' out to the pool, Kasey?' he asked, his white teeth flashing in a huge smile. 'You have a swim for me, it's sure hot enough for it.'

Kasey had started down the steps when Jessie came hurrying out through the door. 'Ah, I've caught you, Jodan. There's a call for you. Someone called Terry Joseph wants to talk to you.'

Jodan hadn't moved, and even when Jessie spoke he stood for a moment longer staring into the hot hazy distance. 'Thanks, Jessie. I'd better take it,' he said tiredly, and went inside.

'I hope it's not bad news.' Jessie frowned. 'The young man on the phone sounded a little perturbed.'

Kasey came back up the steps. 'I hope David, Jodan's brother, is all right.'

Jessie nodded and they both went into the house. Jodan was replacing the receiver when they joined him in the living-room. He continued to stand there, his back to them.

'Jodan?' Kasey said softly. 'It isn't David, is it?'

He turned at the sound of her voice and shook his head. 'No. As far as I know David's fine.' He sighed. 'Terry was just keeping me posted about a problem in the Adelaide branch.' He glanced thoughtfully at Jessie. 'That plane bringing Mike's tractor parts this morning, does it take passengers?'

'I guess so,' Jessie replied. 'But do you have to go? We thought you'd be staying until the weekend, until Greg's wedding.'

Jodan's eyes met Kasey's and fell again.

'Still, I suppose your business is important,' Jessie continued. 'I'll just call Norma Main and see if the plane's left Winterwood yet.'

Jodan moved out into the hall, and on leaden feet Kasey followed him.

Don't go! she wanted to cry out to him. Please don't go! 'Is the problem serious?' she asked evenly.

He stopped and turned to face her.

'I mean, will you be able to get back for the——' Kasey paused '—for the weekend?'

'I'm not sure.' He ran one hand around the back of his neck. 'Terry could handle the business problem, but there's something else. Desiree turned up at the office this morning looking for me. She told Terry to tell me she's leaving David.'

CHAPTER ELEVEN

KASEY felt as though all the breath had been knocked out of her body. Desiree! It wasn't the problem at the office that had Jodan set to fly back to the city—it was his sister-in-law. Desiree pulled the strings and Jodan jumped. It would always be that way. Kasey was a prize fool to ever imagine she could change that.

Now Desiree was leaving her husband. She would be free. Kasey felt numb—no pain, no anything. It was as though she was held in limbo.

'I'll have to go back and talk to her,' Jodan was saying.

I'll have to go to her. History was repeating itself. Hasn't he said as much on their wedding night?

'Heaven only knows what sort of mess she's got herself into.' Jodan was still easing the tension in his neck.

'Perhaps Desiree's old enough to get herself out of it too,' Kasey heard herself say, and Jodan's eyes turned on her, narrowed. She laughed, a short, high, almost hysterical sound. 'But no, good old Jodan is always there to bail her out, to come running.'

'Kasey?'

There was a question in his tone, one she couldn't quite understand, didn't even try to identify. She just knew she had to get away from him, escape before she broke down, betrayed herself by begging him not to go, to stay, to love her as much as she loved him. But that would be crying for the moon. He loved Desiree, and always had. She pulled herself together with no little effort.

'Well, as they say, when you've got to go, you've got to go,' she said flippantly. 'And you'd better hurry—I hear the plane approaching now.'

With that she turned on her heel and almost ran down the hall, flew down the steps, grabbing the reins from the startled stockman, mounting her horse and galloping away.

Tears cascaded down her cheeks, blurring the landscape, and she just as suddenly slumped, staying in the saddle by instinct alone. The horse slowed and then eventually stopped, and dropped its head to chew at a clump of dry grass.

Kasey's shoulders shook as sobs racked her body, until eventually she wiped the dampness from her face with her shirtsleeve. She glanced around her, realising she hadn't come far, only halfway up the hill, and she turned back to look at the homestead in time to see the jeep draw up by the small plane. A tall, white-shirted figure left the jeep and crossed to climb into the plane as the jeep started back towards the homestead.

Jodan was going to Desiree. More tears welled and fell. She heard the splutter of the plane's engine before it roared into life. So Desiree had been right that night of the wedding—Jodan always came back to her.

The plane moved off and Kasey blinked back her tears. It was too late now. The small Cessna was at the end of the airstrip, and then it turned. Oh, Jodan, don't go!

The engine roared as the pilot opened the throttle and gave the plane full thrust for take-off. As he released the brakes the plane rolled forward, gathering speed down the length of the runway. The wheels lifted off the ground and then to Kasey's horror it plunged forward, nose into the dusty red earth.

It took mere seconds, but to Kasey, sitting on her horse watching in shocked disbelief, it all seemed to happen in slow motion. The plane had crashed before her very eyes. She couldn't recall the sound, but the sight was printed indelibly in her mind.

Jodan! Curling smoke began to spiral upwards from the fuselage into the hot, dry air. Fire! No, no!

She spurred the surprised horse into a headlong, reckless gallop.

No! Was she really screaming out the word or was it only echoing inside her head? No! No! Not Jodan. Please—not Jodan!

The ride down the hillside took forever, but now she had reined in the horse at the crash site just as the jeep slithered to a stop behind her. Kasey slid from the saddle and the frightened animal shied, galloping off towards the homestead.

Kasey heard someone call her name, but she paid no heed as she raced towards the plane. And Jodan.

'Jodan!' she called hysterically as she ran, repeating his name over and over.

A figure in a white shirt slid awkwardly out of the crashed aeroplane, stumbled and fell to the ground to lie motionless.

'Jodan!'

Running feet passed her and at the same time someone tackled her from behind, knocking her to the dusty ground.

'Don't move, you crazy little fool!' someone said in her ear, his weight heavy upon her body.

She gasped for breath, tried to lift herself free, but strong arms pushed her face back into the dirt. Dust went up her nose, into her mouth, but before she could so much as splutter a loud explosion rolled deafeningly over them.

When Kasey came to she was lying on the hard wooden veranda at the homestead. Why was she stretched out on the floor? Had she fainted? She tried to move and flinched. Her body felt bruised and achy. She opened her mouth and gritty dirt rasped her teeth. She must have fallen... No! She'd been knocked down.

It all came back in a rush. The plane crash. The fire. Jodan! Oh, no. Jodan lying on the ground—and then the explosion.

Tears trickled down her cheeks, leaving tracks in the dust, as she struggled to sit up. 'Jodan!'

'Ssh! Lie still, love,' Jessie soothed, her hands gently pressing Kasey back before she began wiping her face with a damp cloth. She held a glass to Kasey's lips, insisting she rinse her mouth with water.

'Oh, Jessie,' Kasey cried desperately, 'Jodan—is he...?'

A strong arm slipped beneath her shoulders, drew her against a warm, rock-hard chest, pressed her damp face into a dust-streaked white shirt.

'He can't be dead,' she sobbed pleadingly. She could smell the musky, masculine fragrance of him, feel his arms securely around her.

'Kasey, don't cry, darling. Don't cry.'

She could even hear his voice. She gulped, her body tensing, and she slowly raised her head, blinking the tears from her eyes. 'Jodan?' she got out, and she lifted her hand to his face, touched his jaw, ran her fingers over his cheek, his nose, his mouth. His beautiful mouth. 'Oh, Jodan,' she breathed. 'I thought you were——'

His finger on her lips stopped her and his eyes met hers, blazed, set her aflame. Then he was slowly lowering his mouth to hers. He kissed her gently at first, almost reverently, then quick, soft kisses, until her hand slid around the back of his head and she held him fast, her lips crushing his.

His arms bound her to him as he kissed her again and again, deep, passionate, urgent, drugging kisses, until they collapsed breathlessly against each other.

'I've heard of mouth-to-mouth resuscitation, but this is ridiculous!' Jessie's amused voice reminded them they weren't alone.

'But who...? Oh, Jodan, I was sure... I saw the smoke...' Kasey's fingers tightened on Jodan's arm.

'An awful business, and one that could have been tragic.' Jessie shook her head. 'Your father's inside radioing the flying doctor. The young pilot has a few burns from the fire and we think he may have broken his ankle. He's been very lucky. Now, enough of this. Let's get you cleaned up, Kasey. I think you'd better carry her inside, Jodan.'

He went to lift her, but she struggled to her feet. 'I can walk.' She swayed against him. 'I think.' She glanced down at her jeans and shirt and tried to brush some of the dust from them.

'Don't worry about that,' Jessie admonished. 'They'll wash. You both need a shower and then it's off to bed with you, my girl.'

'Oh, Jessie, I'm fine,' Kasey began.

'I said bed and I mean it. You've had a nasty shock,' Jessie told her firmly. 'I'll send Jodan along with a cup of tea when you're ready.'

In something of a daze Kasey showered and slipped into a soft cotton nightdress. The bed she'd shared with Jodan had been turned down, by Jessie or Jodan, and bore no witness to their fevered lovemaking. Just looking at the bed made her feel weak and all at once terribly confused. With a sigh she sank on to the soft mattress.

Had Jodan really kissed her so passionately in front of Jessie? Or had she been dreaming? She touched her lips and shivered.

There was a tap on the door and then Jodan was inside, closing the door behind him, crossing to set a steaming cup of tea on the table beside the bed. He smelled clean and fresh from his shower and he wore the black robe he'd had on that morning she'd awoken in his bed in his flat in the city.

He was so incredibly attractive. Had her imagination, her desperate wanting, conjured up those moments in his arms, his drugging kisses?

Her eyes were drawn upwards over the tie of his robe, hesitated momentarily on the light mat of dark hair where the lapels of his robe parted, moved to his throat, his firm chin, that mouth, his nose, and finally to his eyes. It was then that she knew it had been no dream.

He slowly sat on the bed beside her, his eyes not leaving hers. He rested one hand on either side of her, then he slowly shook his head and gathered her into his arms, holding her close.

Kasey murmured deep in her throat as she breathed in his familiar fragrance, as her hands roved over his solid, muscular back. 'I thought you'd been killed,' she said, and her voice caught in her throat on a sob. 'When I saw you fall out of the crashed plane and lie there on the ground, I thought——' Kasey shook her head.

Jodan drew away from her, so he could look into her eyes. His hands cupped her face, the pad of his thumb gently caressing her trembling lips.

'That wasn't me, Kasey,' he said softly.

'But I saw... I thought...'

'That was the pilot,' he told her. 'When you raced off I just stood in the hallway trying to tell myself you weren't jealous of Desiree, that I was simply reading jealousy into what you'd said because I wanted to believe it. Because if you were jealous it meant you just might care for me. How I wanted to believe it, Kasey!'

He took a deep, shaky breath. 'You'll never know how much I wanted that.'

Kasey stared at him, scarcely daring to believe what he was saying.

'I wanted it so badly, Kasey, I decided to throw my pride out the window. You see, I followed you up here to Akoonah Downs to offer to set you free, because I couldn't bear having you so close to me and not declaring my love for you every minute of the day. And night.'

Kasey's heartbeats were beginning to behave very erratically.

'When David had his heart attack I had to use my work-load as an excuse to keep away from you,' he went on, 'because I knew if I was near you I'd have to hold you, make love to you. And you gave me every indication that that was the last thing you wanted.' He gave her a crooked smile. 'I thought I was making some headway the night of the Mendelsons' party, but you locked your door against me. That was my lowest ebb, Kasey.

'So I came out to offer you the chance of a divorce. But after I'd made the crazy suggestion I wanted to have you accept it even less. I couldn't go back, Kasey, not without a fight, without pleading my cause.

'And when you raced off you gave me just a small glimmer of hope. I clung to that like a limpet. I was coming after you, to tell you how much I loved you, to beg you to give me a chance to prove it to you. I was just about to mount my horse when the plane crashed.' He grimaced. 'The next thing I knew you were galloping towards the plane so damn recklessly my blood ran cold. I tried to head you off while Billy got the jeep, but you just kept on going. I could see the smoke, the flames. I had to get to you before——' He shook his head, pain crossing his face.

'*You* knocked me down?' Kasey realised suddenly.

'It was the only way I could stop you. I knew the plane was about to blow. I couldn't let anything happen to you.' He leant forward and kissed her reverently. 'I love you so much, my darling,' he said softly, sincerely.

Kasey sighed, her arms sliding around him. 'Oh, Jodan, I love you too. But I just can't believe... I didn't even begin to suspect... And our marriage, it was——'

'The manoeuvre of a desperate man,' he finished for her.

Kasey drew back to gaze at him in wonder.

'Oh, yes. A very desperate man.' He kissed the tip of her nose. 'I wanted it to be strictly conventional, I wanted to court you, propose on bended knee, all the trappings, but you were so elusive, Ice Maiden. If I'd had my way I'd have spirited you off the first night I saw you at that charity "do".

'I fell for you like a ton of bricks, and that hadn't ever happened to me before.' He laughed derisively. 'I'd always prided myself on being pretty suave, very sophisticated, a man about town, but one look at you, that fiery hair, those incredible eyes—well, I fell apart. I was as gauche, as inarticulate as any adolescent. I got Betty Cable to introduce us, but you didn't want to know me no matter how often I tried to get close to you.'

Kasey's eyes fell and her finger played with the dark curls on his chest. 'I was—at the time, I was very mixed up,' she began.

'Because of Parker?' he asked softly, and she met his gaze and nodded.

'I'd imagined I was in love with Greg since I was little more than a child, and I just took it for granted he felt the same way. I thought we'd marry and continue to live here on the Downs. I came to the city when he told me he was going to marry Paula. I suppose I ran away. For those first few months I guess I was a little crazy, literally existing day by day.

'Then, just when I was starting to come out of it, Greg came to see me. He told me he loved me, that he missed me. I thought he'd broken his engagement.' She shrugged. 'He hadn't, and he didn't intend to break it. But he wanted me too.' She looked up at him. 'That was the night I turned up at the tavern. I only had two drinks, but I'm not used to hard alcohol and I hadn't eaten, so I'm afraid the drinks went to my head.

'I had some crazy notion that I needed to have a husband to show off to Greg. Looking back, I can see just how ridiculous it was. I'm so sorry, Jodan.'

'I'm not, Kasey. And I sure as hell wasn't when I offered myself as a husband. It was no coincidence I was at the hotel with your friends that night. I shadowed them, forced myself on them, hoping to see you. I'd been doing that every opportunity I had. That night when you weren't there I very nearly gave up and went home.

'Then you walked in and I couldn't believe my luck.' He shook his head. 'And I still couldn't seem to say the right thing, could I? Everything I said and did antagonised you.'

Kasey chuckled. 'I was livid when you bought me the lemonade! And then to add insult to injury I passed out on you.'

'Oh, Kasey!' He leant his forehead against hers. 'Was ever a man tested during those long dark hours? And when you finally woke up you couldn't remember I'd accepted your proposal of marriage. I had to prompt you.'

'Did you really think I'd go through with it?' she asked him.

He smoothed back her hair, kissed her again. 'I spent the whole time in abject terror that you'd call it off. Right up to the moment the organist began to play the Bridal March, until you signed the register. I was totally disarmed, and completely defenceless.'

'You hid that very well,' Kasey told him drily.

'Oh, the signs were there, Kasey, my love. I fell all over myself, doing the wrong things, saying the wrong things. Especially on our wedding night.' He closed his eyes for long seconds. 'I'll never forgive myself for that, Kasey. I never intended to make love to you that night. I wanted us to get to know each other better, so you'd come to relax with me. You were all tense and wide-eyed, expecting me to spring on you at any moment.

'It was hard to take, Kasey, and I know it's no excuse, but I only meant to tease you, teach you a lesson. But I hadn't allowed for my wanting you so badly. I was going to kiss you, let you think the worst and then roll over and go to sleep. With a king-sized fool I was! I couldn't seem to stop myself. I behaved like a selfish oaf, and I'm truly sorry.'

Kasey smiled shyly at him. 'You more than made up for it this morning,' she said softly, and his eyes blazed.

'I thought I'd lost you forever,' his voice was thick, 'killed any small hope you'd learn to love me.'

'I was half in love with you before we were married, but I was so mixed up and even a little guilty about Greg. I guess my feelings for him had become something of a habit and I didn't feel I could admit to myself I wanted you.'

'What fools we were! And what a way to start a honeymoon—everything going wrong, my behaviour, all topped off with Desiree's call.'

Kasey stiffened. Desiree. She'd forgotten about Desiree. He couldn't still love Desiree after all he'd just told her. Could he?

'Kasey?' Jodan sat back from her, held her gaze, his hands on her shoulders tightening. 'Kasey, what is it? Don't freeze me out. Not now.'

'It's——' She swallowed. 'It's Desiree. Do you ... Are you and Desiree... I overheard you at your parents' wedding anniversary. And then at our wedding Desiree told me you always come back to her,' she finished in a rush.

Jodan expelled the breath he'd been holding. 'Desiree's got a problem. Every so often she strays, gets fed up with marriage and goes off with whoever's there and available. She's let David a merry dance over the years, and I feel somewhat responsible.

'I met her when I was at university, and I fancied I was in love with her. I took her home to meet my parents and my brother. She found out David was the elder son, our father's heir, so to speak, and as I was just starting my own business she dropped me cold and set her sights on David.

'At the time I was upset and I turned all my energies into making Caine Computers a success, initially to show her how mistaken she'd been, but I soon realised I was lucky to have been let off the hook.

'About the time I first met you Desiree decided she was bored again, and that it would be fun to pick up where she'd left off with me. She got pretty persistent, and I hoped the fact that I was marrying you would put an end to her childish games. When it didn't I thought if I just kept her at arm's length she'd eventually tire of it and find someone else. But what I felt for Desiree died before she even married David. Please believe that, Kasey.'

She looked into his eyes and saw the love she had never dare to dream he would feel for her reflected there, and she smiled, knowing at last she was free of her sister-in-law.

Jodan's gaze roamed her face, drinking in each feature. 'What you do to me, Mrs Caine!' He gave a rueful smile. 'I have another confession too.'

Kasey raised her eyebrows, her heartbeats beginning to thunder at the look in his eyes.

'This morning when I suggested you consider the possibility you might be pregnant, I was so desperate for you not to leave me I was hoping we had made a baby.'

'We might have,' Kasey admitted huskily.

'Would you mind?' he asked, his voice uneven.

Kasey shook her head. 'How could I mind? I love you, Jodan. I want to have our children, watch them grow, share your life and grow old with you.'

Slowly Jodan lowered his head, his lips tenderly claiming hers, hardening, setting fire to her senses, fanning the flame until it raced unchecked through her body. And somehow they were lying back on the bed, Jodan's lips seeking the mound of her breast.

He paused, looked up at her suddenly, his fingers gently running over the bruise she'd noticed earlier. 'I did this?' he asked thickly, and she smiled.

'It doesn't matter,' she told him breathlessly.

'I'll have to be more careful in future,' he began, and she silenced him with her lips.

This time their lovemaking was quick, urgent, and afterwards they lay sated, bodies moulded together, languidly entwined.

Jodan raised himself on one elbow to gaze down at her, his blue eyes warm and filled with love. 'There's just one small thing, Mrs Caine.'

Kasey's fingers probed the hollow of his spine and he moaned softly, deep in his throat. 'What's that, Mr Caine?' she asked lazily, a small, satisfied smile lifting the corners of her mouth.

'Does this mean,' he watched her fingers as they trailed across his hip to circle his navel, 'that I can assume the divorce is off?' he finished on a groan, and Kasey laughed softly, her fingers caressing, her lips meeting his in a kiss that left little doubt that his assumption was perfectly correct.

PENNY JORDAN

**Sins and infidelities...
Dreams and obsessions...
Shattering secrets
unfold in...**

THE HIDDEN YEARS

SAGE — stunning, sensual and
vibrant, she spent a lifetime
distancing herself from a past too
painful to confront... the mother
who seemed to hold her at bay,
the father who resented her and
the heartache of unfulfilled love.
To the world, Sage was
independent and invulnerable—
but it was a mask she cultivated to
hide a desperation she herself
couldn't quite understand...
until an unforeseen turn of events
drew her into the discovery of the
hidden years, finally allowing
Sage to open her heart to a
passion denied for so long.

The Hidden Years—a compelling novel of truth and passion
that will unlock the heart and soul of every woman.

AVAILABLE IN OCTOBER!
Watch for your opportunity to complete your Penny Jordan set.
POWER PLAY and SILVER will also be available in October.

HIDDEN

This October, Harlequin offers you a second
two-in-one collection of romances

A SPECIAL
SOMETHING

THE FOREVER
INSTINCT

by the award-winning author,

Barbara Delinsky

Now, two of Barbara Delinsky's most loved books are
available together in this special edition that new and
longtime fans will want to add to their bookshelves.

Let Barbara Delinsky double your reading pleasure with
her memorable love stories, A SPECIAL SOMETHING and
THE FOREVER INSTINCT.

Available wherever Harlequin books are sold.   TWO-D

HARLEQUIN

Romance

**This October,
travel to England with
Harlequin Romance
FIRST CLASS title #3155
TRAPPED
by Margaret Mayo**

''I'm my own boss now and I intend to stay that way.''

Candra Drake loved her life of freedom on her narrow-boat
home and was determined to pursue her career as a company
secretary free from the influence of any domineering man.
Then enigmatic, arrogant Simeon Sterne breezed into her life,
forcing her to move and threatening a complete takeover of her
territory and her heart....